Both girls gasped and stared incredulously

The Boarded-Up House

Augusta Huiell Seaman

With the Original Illustrations by
C. Clyde Squires

DOVER PUBLICATIONS, INC.
Mineola, New York

Bibliographical Note

This Dover edition, first published by Dover Publications, Inc., in 2014, is an unabridged republication of the work originally published by the Century Co., New York, in 1915.

International Standard Book Number

ISBN-13: 978-0-486-78188-4
ISBN-10: 0-486-78188-7

Manufactured in the United States by Courier Corporation
78188701   2014
www.doverpublications.com

CONTENTS

LIST OF ILLUSTRATIONS

The Boarded-Up House

THE
BOARDED-UP HOUSE

CHAPTER I

GOLIATH LEADS THE WAY

CYNTHIA sat on her veranda steps, chin in hand, gazing dolefully at the gray September sky. All day, up to half an hour before, the sky had been cloudlessly blue, the day warm and radiant. Then, all of a sudden, the sun had slunk shamefacedly behind a high rising bank of cloud, and its retiring had been accompanied by a raw, chilly wind. Cynthia scowled. Then she shivered. Then she pulled the collar of her white sweater up to her ears and buttoned it over. Then she muttered something about "wishing Joy would hurry, for it's going to rain!" Then she dug her hands into her sweater pockets and stared across the lawn at a blue hydrangea bush with a single remaining bunch of blossoms hanging heavy on its stem.

Suddenly there was a flash of red on a veranda farther down the street, and a long, musical whistle. Cynthia jumped up and waved madly. The flash of red, speeding toward her, developed into a bright red sweater, cap, and skirt.

"Don't scold! Now you must n't be cross, Cynthia. Anne was just putting a big batch of sugar-cookies in the oven, and I simply *had* to wait till they were done! I 've brought a lot over for you. Here!" The owner of the red sweater crammed a handful of hot cookies into Cynthia's pocket.

"You did keep me waiting an age, Joy," Cynthia began, struggling with a mouthful of cooky; "but I forgive you. I 'd almost begun to be—angry!" Joy (her right name was Joyce) ignored the latter remark.

"We can't go! Momsie positively forbade it. Why on earth could n't it have kept sunny a little longer? It 'll rain any minute now, I suppose."

4

"I know," Cynthia sympathized. "Mother forbade me too, long before you came out. And we counted on it so! Won't be much more chance to go canoeing *this* season." They sat down listlessly on the veranda steps, and solaced themselves with the last remnants of the cookies. Life appeared a trifle drab, as it usually does when cherished plans are demolished and the sun goes in! Very shortly there were no more cookies.

"What on earth has happened to your hydrangea bush? It was full of blossoms yesterday," Joyce suddenly exclaimed.

"Bates's pup!" replied Cynthia, laconically. There was no need of further explanation. Joyce giggled at its shorn appearance, and then relapsed into another long silence. There were times when these two companions could talk frantically for hours on a stretch. There were other seasons when they would sit silent yet utterly understanding one another for equally prolonged periods. They had been bosom friends from babyhood, as their parents had been before them. Shoulder to shoulder they had gone through kindergarten and day-school together, and were now abreast in their first high-school year. Even their birthdays fell in the same month. And the only period of the year which saw them parted was the few weeks during vacation when their respective parents (who had different tastes in summer resorts) dragged them unwillingly away to mountain and sea-shore. Literally, nothing else ever separated them save the walls of their own dwellings—and the Boarded-up House.

It is now high time to introduce the Boarded-up House, which has been staring us out of countenance ever since this story began! For the matter of that, it had stared the two girls out of countenance ever since they came to live in the little town of Rockridge, one on each side of it. And long before they came there, long before ever they were born, or Rockridge had begun its mushroom growth as a pretty, modern, country town, the Boarded-up House had stared the passers-by out of countenance with almost irritating persistence.

It was set well back from the street, in a big

inclosure guarded by a very rickety picket-fence, and a gate that was never shut but hung loosely on one hinge. Unkempt bushes and tall, rank grass flourished in this inclosure, and near the porch grew two pine-trees like sentinels at the entrance. At the back was a small orchard of ancient cherry-trees, and near the rear door a well-curb, with the great sweep half rotted away.

The house itself was a big, rambling affair of the Colonial type, with three tall pillars supporting the veranda roof and reaching above the second story. On each side of the main part was a generous wing. It stood rather high on a sloping lawn, and we have said that it "stared" at passers-by—with truth, because very near the roof were two little windows shaped like half-circles. They somehow bore a close resemblance to a pair of eyes that stared and stared and *stared* with calm, unwinking blankness.

As to the other windows and doors, they were all tightly boarded up. The boards in the big front door had a small door fashioned in them, and this door fastened with a very rusty lock. No one ever came in or out. No one ever tended the grounds. The place had been without an occcupant for years. The Boarded-up House had always been boarded up, as long as its neighbors could recollect. It was not advertised for sale. When the little town of Rockridge began to build up, people speculated about it for a while with considerable interest. But as they could never obtain any definite information about it, they finally gave it up, and accepted the queer old place as a matter of course.

To Cynthia Sprague and Joyce Kenway, it had, when they first came to live on either side of it, some five years before, afforded for a while an endless source of attraction. They had played house on the broad veranda, climbed the trees in the orchard, organized elaborate games of hide-and-seek among the thick, high bushes that grew so close to the walls, and in idle moments had told each other long stories about its former (imaginary) inmates. But as they grew older and more absorbed in outside affairs, their interest in it ceased, till at length it came to be only a source of irritation to them, since it separated their homes by a wide space that they considered rather a nuisance to have to traverse.

So they sat, on this threatening afternoon, cheated of their anticipated canoe-trip on the little stream that threaded its way through their town to the wide Sound,—sat munching sugar-cookies, glowering at the weather, and thinking of nothing very special. Suddenly there was a flash of gray across the lawn, closely pursued by a streak of yellow. Both girls sprang to their feet, Joyce exclaiming indignantly:

"Look at Bates's pup chasing Goliath!" The latter individual was the Kenways' huge Maltese cat, well deserving of his name in appearance, but not in nature, for he was known to be the biggest coward in cat-dom. The girls stood on tiptoe to watch the chase. Over the lawn and through an opening in the picket-fence of the Boarded-up House sped Goliath, his enemy yapping at his heels, and into the tangled thicket of bushes about the nearer wing. Into the bushes also plunged Bates's pup, and there ensued the sound of sundry, baffled yelps. Then, after a moment, Bates's pup emerged, one ear comically cocked, and ambled away in search of other entertainment. Nothing else happened, and the girls resumed their seat on the veranda steps. Presently Joyce remarked, idly:

"Does it strike you as queer, Cynthia, what could have become of Goliath?"

"Not at all," replied Cynthia, who had no special gift of imagination. "What *could* have happened to him? I suppose he climbed into the bushes."

"He could n't have done that without being in reach of the pup," retorted Joyce. "And he could n't have come out either side, or we 'd have seen him. Now where can he be? I vote we go and look him up!" She had begun with but a languid interest, seeking only to pass the time, and had suddenly ended up with tremendous enthusiasm. That was like Joyce.

10

GOLIATH LEADS THE WAY

"I don't see what you want to do that for,"
argued Cynthia. "I don't care what became
of him as long as he got away from Bates's
pup, and I'm very comfortable right here!"
Cynthia was large and fair and plump, and inclined to be a little indolent.

"But don't you see," insisted Joyce, "that
he must have hidden in some strange place,—
and one he must have known about, too, for
he went straight to it! I'm just curious to
find out his 'bunk.'" Joyce was slim and dark
and elfin, full of queer pranks, sudden enthusiastic plans, and very vivid of imagination, a
curious contrast to the placid, slow-moving
Cynthia. Joyce also, as a rule, had her way in
matters, and she had it now.

"Very well!" sighed Cynthia, in slow assent.
"Come on!" They wandered down the steps,
across the lawn, through the gap in the fence,
and tried to part the bushes behind which
Goliath had disappeared. But they were
thick lilac bushes, grown high and rank. Joyce
struggled through them, tearing the pocket
of her sweater and pulling her hair awry.

11

Cynthia prudently remained on the outskirts. The quest did not greatly interest her.

"There's nothing back there but the foundation of the house," she remarked.

"You're wrong. There is!" called back Joy, excitedly, from the depths. "Crawl around the end of the bushes, Cyn! It will be easier. I want to show you something." There was so much suppressed mystery in Joy's voice that Cynthia obeyed without demur, and back of the bushes found her examining a little boarded-up window into the cellar. One board of it had, through age and dampness, rotted and fallen away. There happened to be no glass window-frame behind it.

"Here's where Goliath disappeared," whispered Joyce, "and he's probably in there now!" Cynthia surveyed the hole unconcernedly.

"That's so," she agreed. "He will probably come out after a while. Now that you've discovered his 'bunk,' I hope you're coming back to the veranda. We might have a game of tennis, too, before it rains." Joyce sat back on her heels, and looked her companion straight in the eye.

"Cynthia," she said, in a tense whisper, "did it ever occur to you that there's something *strange* about the Boarded-up House?"

"No," declared Cynthia, honestly, "it never did. I never thought about it."

"Well, I have—sometimes, at least—and once in a long while, do you know, I've even dreamed I was exploring it. Look here, Cynthia, wouldn't you *like* to explore it? I'm just crazy to!" Cynthia stared and shrugged her shoulders.

"Mercy, no! It would be dark and musty and dirty. Besides, we've no business in there. We'd be trespassers. What ever made you think of it? There's probably nothing to see, anyway. It's an empty house."

"That's just where you're mistaken!" retorted Joyce. "I heard Father say once that it was furnished throughout, and left exactly as it was,—so some one told him, some old lady, I think he said. It's a Colonial mansion, too, and stood here before the Revolution. There was n't any town of Rockridge, you know, till just recently,—only the turnpike road off there where Warrington Avenue is now. This house was the only one around, for a long distance."

"Well, that sounds interesting, but, even still, I don't see why you want to get inside, anyhow. I 'm perfectly satisfied with the outside. And, more than that, we could n't get in if we tried. So there!" If Cynthia imagined she had ended the argument with Joyce by any such reasoning, she was doomed to disappointment. Joyce shrugged her shoulders with a disgusted movement.

"I never saw any one like you, Cynthia Sprague! You 've absolutely *no* imagination! Don't you see how Goliath got in? Well, I could get in the same way, and so could you!" She gave the boards a sharp pull, and succeeded in dislodging another. "Five minutes' work will clear this window, and then—"

"But good gracious, Joy, you would n't break in a window of a strange house and climb in the cellar like a burglar!" cried Cynthia, genuinely shocked.

"I just would! Why, it's an *adventure*, Cynthia, like the kind we've always longed for. You know we've always said we'd love to have some adventures, above everything else. And we *never* have, and now here's one right under our noses!" Joyce was almost tearful in her earnestness to convince the doubting Cynthia. And then Cynthia yielded, as she always did, to Joy's entreaties.

"Very well. It is an adventure, I suppose. But why not wait till some bright, sunny day? It'll be horridly dark and gloomy in there this afternoon."

"Nonsense!" cried Joyce, who never could bear to wait an instant in carrying out some cherished plan. "Run back to your house, Cynthia, and smuggle out a candle and a box of matches. And *don't* let any one see what you take!" But this Cynthia flatly refused to do, urging that she would certainly be discovered and held up for instant explanation by the lynx-eyed Bridget who guarded the kitchen.

15

"Very well, then. I'll have to get them from mine, I suppose. Anne never asks what I'm doing," said Joyce, resignedly. "You stay here and wait!" She sped away toward her own house, but was soon back, matches and candle under her sweater, her hands full of fresh cookies.

"We'll eat these when we're inside. Here, stuff them into your pockets! And help me break these other boards away. My! but they're rotten!" Cynthia helped, secretly very reluctant and fearful of consequences, and they soon had the little window free of obstructions. Joyce poked in her head and peered about.

"It's as dark as a pocket, but I see two things like balls of fire,—that's Goliath up on a beam, I suppose. It is n't far to the ground. Here goes!" She slipped in, feet first, let herself down, hung on to the sill a moment, then disappeared from view.

"Oh, Joyce!" gasped Cynthia, sticking her head through the opening into the dark, "where *are* you?"

16

"Right here!" laughed Joyce from below. "Trying to light the candle. Come along! The stones of the wall are like regular steps. You can put your feet on 'em!"

"Oh, but the *mice,* and the *spiders,* and—and all sorts of things!" groaned Cynthia. "I 'm afraid of them!"

"Nonsense! *they* can't hurt you!" replied Joyce, unsympathetically. "If you don't come soon, I 'm going on. I 'm so impatient to see things, I can't wait. You 'd better hurry up, if you 're coming."

"But it is n't *right!* It 's trespassing!" cried Cynthia, making her last stand. Joyce scorned to argue further along this line.

"We talked that all over before. Good-by! I 'm off! I 've got the candle lit." Cynthia suddenly surrendered.

"Oh, wait, wait! I 'm coming!" She adopted Joyce's mode of ingress, but found it scarcely as easy as it looked, and her feet swung in space, groping wildly for the steps described.

"I 'm stuck! I can't move! Oh, why am I so fat and clumsy!" she moaned. Joyce laughed, placed her companion's feet on a ledge, and hauled her down, breathless, cobwebby, and thoroughly scared.

The lighted candle threw but a feeble illumination on the big, bare space they stood in. The beams overhead were thick with cobwebs, hanging like gray portières from every projection. Otherwise the inclosure was clear, except for a few old farm implements in a distant corner. As Joyce raised the candle over her head, a flight of stairs could be dimly discerned.

"This way!" she ordered, and they moved toward it cautiously. At that moment, there came from behind them a sudden scratching and scrambling, and then a thud. Both girls uttered a low, frightened shriek and clung together. But it was only Goliath, disturbed in his hiding-place. They turned in time to see him clambering through the window.

"Joyce, this is horrid!" gasped Cynthia. "My heart is beating like a trip-hammer. Let's go back."

"It's lovely!" chuckled Joyce. "It's what

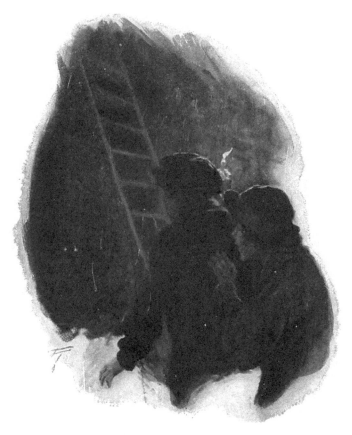

A flight of stairs could be dimly discerned

GOLIATH LEADS THE WAY

I 've always longed for. I feel like Christopher Columbus! I would n't go back now for worlds! And to think we 've neglected such a mystery at our front doors, as you might say, all these years!" And she dragged the protesting Cynthia toward the cellar stairs.

CHAPTER II

IN SEARCH OF ADVENTURE

THEY stumbled up the cellar steps, their eyes growing gradually used to the semi-darkness. At the top was a shut door which refused to be moved, and they feared for a moment that failure awaited them in this early period of the voyage of discovery. But after some vigorous pushing and rattling, it gave with an unexpected jerk, and they were landed pell-mell into a dark hallway.

"Now," declared Joyce, "this is the beginning of something interesting, I hope!" Cynthia said nothing, having, indeed, much ado to appear calm and hold herself from making a sudden bolt back to the cellar window. With candle held high, Joyce proceeded to investigate their surroundings. They seemed to be in a wide, central hall running through the

house from front to back. A generous stairway of white-painted wood with slender ma-
hogany railing ascended to an upper floor.
Some large paintings and portraits hung on
the walls, but the candle did not throw enough
light to permit seeing them well. The furniture in the hall consisted of several tall,
straight-backed chairs set at intervals against
the walls, and at one side a massive table covered thick with the dust of years. There was
a distinctly old-fashioned, "different" air about
the place, but nothing in any other way remarkable.

"You see!" remarked Cynthia. "There
is n't anything wonderful here, and the air is
simply horrid. I hope you 're satisfied. *Do*
come back!"

"But we have n't seen a quarter of it yet!
This is only the hall. Now for the room on the
right!" Joyce hauled open a pair of closed
folding-doors, and held the candle above her
head. If they were searching for things
strange and inexplicable, here at last was their
reward! Both girls gasped and stared in-

credulously, first at the scene before them, then at each other.

The apartment was a dining-room. More portraits and paintings shone dimly from the walls. A great candelabrum hung from the ceiling, with sconces for nearly a hundred candles and ornamented with glittering crystal pendants. An enormous sideboard occupied almost an entire end of the room. In the middle, a long dining-table stood under the candelabrum.

But here was the singular feature. The table was still set with dishes, as though for a feast. And the chairs about it were all pushed awry, and some were overturned. Napkins, yellowed with age, were fallen about, dropped apparently in sudden forgetfulness. The china and glassware stood just as they had been left, though every ancient vestige of food had long since been carried away by the mice.

As plain as print, one could read the signs of some feasting party interrupted and guests hastily leaving their places to return no more. The girls understood it in a flash.

"But why—why," said Joyce, speaking her thought aloud, "was it all left just like this? Why were n't things cleared up and put away? What could have happened? Cynthia, this is the strangest thing I ever heard of!" Cynthia only stared, and offered no explanation. Plainly, she was impressed at last.

"Come on!" half whispered Joyce, "Let's see the room across the hall. I'm crazy to explore it all!" Together they tiptoed to the other side of the hall. A kind of awe had fallen upon them. There was more here than even Joyce had hoped or imagined. This was a house of mystery.

The apartment across the hall proved to be the drawing-room. Though in evident disarray it, however, exhibited fewer signs of the strange, long-past agitation. In dimensions it was similar to the dining-room, running from front to back of the house. Here, too, was another elaborate candelabrum, somewhat smaller than the first, queer, spindle-legged, fiddle-backed chairs, beautiful cabinets and tables, and an old, square piano, still open. The chairs stood in irregular groups of twos and threes, chumming cozily together as their occupants had doubtless done, and over the piano had been carelessly thrown a long, filmy silk scarf, one end hanging to the floor. Upon everything the dust was indescribably thick, and cobwebs hung from the ceiling.

"Do you know," spoke Joyce, in a whisper, after they had looked a long time, "I think I can guess part of an explanation for all this. There was a party here, long, long ago,—perhaps a dinner-party. Folks had first been sitting in the drawing-room, and then went to the dining-room for dinner. Suddenly, in the midst of the feast, something happened,—I can't imagine what,—but it broke up the good time right away. Every one jumped up from the table, upsetting chairs and dropping napkins. Perhaps they all rushed out of the room. Anyway, they never came back to finish the meal. And after that, the owner shut the house and boarded it up and went away, never stopping to clear up or put things to rights. Awfully sudden, that, and awfully queer!"

"Goodness, Joy! You're as good as a detective! How did you ever think all that out?" murmured Cynthia, admiringly.

"Why, it's very simple," said Joyce. "The drawing-room is all right,—just looks like any other parlor where a lot of people have been sitting, before it was put to rights. But the dining-room's different. Something happened there, suddenly, and people just got their things on and left, after that! Can't you see it? But what *could* it have been? Oh, I'd give my *eyes* to know, Cynthia!

"See here!" she added, after a moment's thought. "I've the loveliest idea! You just spoke of detectives, and that put it into my head. Let's play we're detectives, like Sherlock Holmes, and ferret out this mystery. It will be the greatest lark ever! We will come here often, and examine every bit of evidence we can find, and gather information outside if we can, and put two and two together, and see if we can't make out the whole story. Oh, it's gorgeous! Did two girls ever have such an adventure before!" She clasped her hands

27

ecstatically, first having presented the candle to Cynthia, because she was too excited to hold it. Even the placid and hitherto objecting Cynthia was fired by the scheme.

"Yes, let's!" she assented. "I'll ask Mother if she knows anything about this old place."

"No you won't!" cried Joyce, coming suddenly to earth. "This has got to be kept a strict secret. Never *dare* to breathe it! Never speak of this house at all! Never show the slightest interest in it! And we must come here often. Do you want folks to suspect what we are doing and put a stop to it all? It's all right, *really,* of course. We're not doing any actual wrong or harming anything. But they wouldn't understand."

"Very well, then," agreed Cynthia, meekly, cowed but bewildered. "I don't see, though, how you're going to find out things if you don't ask."

"You must get at it in other ways," declared Joyce, but did not explain the process just then.

IN SEARCH OF ADVENTURE

"This candle will soon be done for!" suddenly announced the practical Cynthia. "Why did n't you bring a bigger one?"

"Could n't find any other," said Joyce. "Let's finish looking around here and leave the rest for another day." They began accordingly to walk slowly about the room, peering up at the pictures on the walls and picking their way with care around the furniture without moving or touching anything. Presently they came abreast of the great open fireplace. A heavy chair was standing directly in front of it, but curiously enough, with its back to what must have been once a cheery blaze. They moved around it carefully and bent to examine the pretty Delft tiles that framed the yawning chimney-place, below the mantel. Then Joyce stepped back to look at the plates and vases on the mantel. Suddenly she gave a little cry:

"Hello! That's *queer!* Look, Cynthia!" Cynthia, still studying the tiles, straightened up to look where her companion had pointed. But in that instant the dying candle-flame sputtered, flickered, and *went out,* leaving only a small mass of warm tallow in Cynthia's hand. For a moment, there was horrified silence. The heavy darkness seemed to cast a spell over even the irrepressible Joyce. But not for long.

"Too bad!" she began. "Where are the matches, Cynthia? I handed them to you. We can light our way out by them." Cynthia produced the box from the pocket of her sweater and opened it.

"Mercy! There are only three left!" she cried, feeling round in it.

"Never mind. They will light us out of this room and through the hall to the cellar stairs. When we get there the window will guide us."

Cynthia struck the first match, and they hurriedly picked their way around the scattered furniture. But the match went out before they reached the door. The second saw them out of the room and into the long hall. The third, alas! broke short off at its head, and proved useless. Then a real terror of the dark, unknown spaces filled them both. Breathless, frantic, they felt their way along the walls, groping blindly for the elusive cellar door. At length Joyce's hand struck a knob.

"Here it is!" she breathed. They pulled open the door and plunged through it, only to find themselves in some sort of a closet, groping among musty clothes that were hanging there.

"Oh, it is n't, it is n't!" wailed Cynthia. "Oh, I 'll never, never come into this dreadful house again!" But Joyce had regained her poise.

"It 's all right! Our door is just across the hall. I remember where it is now. She pulled the shuddering Cynthia out of the closet, and felt her way across the wide hall space.

"Here it is! Now we are all *serene!*" she cried triumphantly, opening a door which they found gave on a flight of steps. And as they crept down, a dim square of good, honest daylight sent their spirits up with a bound. It was raining great pelting drops as they scrambled out and scampered for Cynthia's veranda. But daylight, even if dismal with rain, had served to restore them completely to their usual gaiety.

"By the way, Joyce," she said, as they stood on the porch shaking the rain from their skirts, "what was it you were pointing at just when the candle went out? I did n't have time to see."

"Why, the *strangest* thing!" whispered Joyce. "There was a big picture hanging over the mantel. But what do you think? It hung there *with its face turned to the wall!*"

CHAPTER III

WHILE Cynthia was bending over her desk during study-hour, struggling with a hopelessly entangled account in Latin of Cæsar and his Gallic Wars, her next neighbor thrust a note into her hand. Glad of any diversion, she opened it and read:

This afternoon for the B. U. H. How much pocket-money have you?

J.

Cynthia had no difficulty in guessing the meaning of the initials, but she could not imagine what pocket-money had to do with the matter, so she wrote back:

All right. Only thirty cents. More next week.

C.

She passed it along to Joyce at the other end of the room, and returned to Cæsar in a more cheerful frame of mind. Joyce, she

33

knew, would explain all mysteries later, and she was content to wait.

Almost a week had passed since the first adventure of the Boarded-up House, and nothing further had happened. Joyce and Cynthia were healthy, normal girls, full of interests connected with their school, with outdoor affairs, and with social life, so they had much to occupy them beside this curious quest on which they had become engaged. A fraternity meeting had occupied one afternoon, dancing-school another, a tramping-excursion a third, and so on through the ensuing week. Not once, however, in the midst of all these outside interests, had they forgotten their strange adventure. When they were alone together they talked of it incessantly, and laid elaborate plans for future amateur detective work.

"It's just like a story!" Joyce would exclaim. "And who would ever have thought of a *story* in that old, Boarded-up House. And *us* in the midst of it!" Cynthia's first question that afternoon, on the way home from high school, was:

"What did you ask about pocket-money for? I'm down pretty low on my allowance, but I don't see what that's got to do with things." Joyce laughed.

"Well, I'm lower yet—ten cents to last till the month's out! But hasn't it struck you that we've got to have *candles*—plenty of them—and matches, and a couple of candlesticks at least? How else can we ever get about the place, pitch-dark as it all is? And if we tried to get them from home, some one would suspect right away."

"Ten cents' worth of candles ought to last us quite a while," began the practical Cynthia; "and ten cents more will buy a whole package of safety-matches. And for five cents we can get a candlestick, but we'd better stop at *one* for the present, or we won't have a cent left between us! Let's get them right now." While they were making their purchases, Cynthia had another idea.

"I'll tell you what, Joyce, I'm going to take along a dust-cloth and clean up around the window where we get in. My sweater was just black with dirt and cobwebs last time, and Mother *almost* insisted on an explanation. Fortunately she was called away for something, just then, and afterward did n't think of it. I 've washed the sweater since!"

"Good idea!" assented Joyce. "Momsie wanted to know how I 'd torn mine and got it so mussy, too. I told her I 'd been chasing up. Goliath,—which was really quite true, you know."

"I never *can* think of things to say that will be the truth and yet not give the whole thing away!" sighed the downright Cynthia. "I wish I were as quick as you!"

"Never mind! You 've got the *sense,* Cynthia! I never would have thought of the dust-cloth."

Getting into the Boarded-up House this time was accompanied by less difficulty than the first. Before entering, Cynthia thoroughly dusted the window-ledge and as far about it as she could reach, with the result that there was less, if any, damage to their clothes. Armed as they were with plenty of candles and matches, there were no shudders either, or fears of the unknown and the dark. Even Cynthia was keen for the quest, and Joyce was simply bursting with new ideas, some of which she expounded to Cynthia as they were lighting their candles in the cellar.

"You know, Cyn, I 've been looking at the place carefully from the outside. We have n't seen a third of it yet,—no, not even a *quarter!* There 's the wing off the parlor toward your house, and the one off the dining-room toward mine. I suppose the kitchen must be in that one, but I can't think what 's in the other, unless it 's a library. We must see these to-day. And then there 's all up-stairs."

"What I want to see most of all is the picture you spoke of that hangs in the parlor," said Cynthia. "Do you suppose we could turn it around?"

"Oh, I 'd love to, only I don't know whether we ought! And it 's heavy, too. I hardly think we could. Perhaps we might just try to peep behind it. You know, Cynthia, I realize we 're doing something a little *queer* being in this house and prying about. I'm not sure our folks would approve of it. Only the old thing has been left *so* long, and there's such a mystery about it, and we're not harming or disturbing anything, that perhaps it isn't so dreadful. Anyhow, we must be *very* careful not to pry into anything we ought not touch. Perhaps then it will be all right." Cynthia agreed to all this without hesitation. She, indeed, had even stronger feelings than Joyce on the subject of their trespassing, but the joy of the adventure and the mystery with which they were surrounding it, outweighed her scruples. When they were half-way up the cellar steps, Joyce, who was ahead, suddenly exclaimed:

"Why, the door is open! Probably we left it so in our hurry the other day. We must be more careful after this, and leave everything as we find it." They tiptoed along the hall with considerably more confidence than on their former visit, pausing to hold their candles up to the pictures, and peeping for a moment into the curiously disarranged dining-room.

But they entered the drawing-room first and stood a long while before the fireplace, gazing up at the picture's massive frame and its challenging wooden back. A heavy, ropelike cord with large silk tassels attached the picture to its hook, and the cord was twisted, as if some one had turned the picture about without stopping to readjust it.

"How strange!" murmured Cynthia. But Joyce had been looking at something else.

"Do you see that big chair with its back close to the mantel?" she exclaimed. "I've been wondering why it stands in that position with its back to the fireplace. There was a fire there. You can tell by the ashes and that half-burned log. Well, don't you see? Some one pulled that chair close to the mantel, stepped on it, and turned the picture face to the wall. Now, I wonder why!"

"But look here!" cried Cynthia. "If some one else stood up there and turned the picture around, why couldn't we do the same? We could turn it back after we'd seen it, couldn't we?" Joyce thought it over a moment.

"I'll tell you, Cynthia (and I suppose you'll think me queer!), there are two reasons why I'd rather not do it right now. In the first place, that silk cord it's hanging by may be awfully rotten after all these years, and if we touch it, the whole thing may fall. And then, somehow, I sort of like to keep the mystery about that picture till a little later,—till we've seen the rest of the house and begun 'putting two and two together.' Wouldn't you?" Cynthia agreed, as she was usually likely to do, and Joyce added:

"Now let's see what's in this next room. I think it must be a library. The door of it opens right into this." Bent on further discovery, they opened the closed door carefully. It was, as Joyce had guessed, a library. Book-shelves completely filled three sides of the room. A long library table with an old-fashioned reading-lamp stood in the middle. The fourth side of the room was practically devoted to another huge fireplace, and over the mantel hung another portrait. It was of a beautiful young woman, and before

40

it the girls stopped, fascinated, to gaze a long while.

There was little or nothing in this room to indicate that any strange happening had transpired here. A few books were strewn about as though they had been pulled out and thrown down hastily, but that was all. The one thing that attracted most strongly was the portrait of the beautiful woman—she seemed scarcely more than a girl—over the fireplace. The two explorers turned to gaze at it afresh.

"There's one thing I've noticed about it that's different from the others," said Joyce, thoughtfully. "It's fresher and more—more modern than the rest of the portraits in the drawing-room and hall. Don't you think so?" Cynthia did.

"And look at her dress, those long, full sleeves and the big, bulging skirt! That's different, too. And then her hair, not high and powdered and all fussed up, but low and parted smooth and drawn down over her ears, and that dear little wreath of tiny roses! She almost seems to be going to speak.

41

And, oh, Cynthia, is n't she beautiful with those big, brown eyes! Somehow I feel as if I just loved her—she 's such a *darling!* And *I* believe she had more to do with the queer things in this house than any of those other dead-and-alive picture-ladies. Tell you what! We 'll go to the public library to-morrow and get out a big book on costumes of the different centuries that I saw there once. Then, by looking up this one, we can tell just about what time she lived. What do you say?"

"As usual, you 've thought of just the thing to do. I never would have," murmured Cynthia, still gazing at the picture of the lovely lady. Suddenly Joyce started nervously:

"Hush! Do you hear anything? I 'm almost certain I heard a sound in the other room!" They both fell to listening intently. Yes, there *was* a sound, a strange, indefinable one like a soft tiptoeing at long intervals, and even a curious, hoarse breathing. Something was certainly outside in the drawing-room.

"What shall we *do?*" breathed Cynthia. "We can't get out of here without passing

They stared with the fascination of horror

through that room! Oh, Joyce!" They listened again. The sound appeared to be approaching the door. It was, without doubt, a soft tiptoeing step. Suddenly there was the noise of a chair scraping on the floor as if it had been accidentally brushed against. Both girls were now numb with terror. They were caught as in a trap. There was no escape. They could only wait in racking suspense where they were.

As they stared with the fascination of horror, the partially open door was pushed farther open and a dim gray form glided around its edge. Joyce clutched Cynthia, gave one little shriek, half-relief and half-laughter, and gasped:

"Oh, Cynthia! *It's Goliath!*"

CHAPTER IV

IT was, indeed, Goliath. He was an enormous cat, and his purr was as oversized as his body. That was the hoarse sound that they had thought was heavy breathing. His footfalls too could be distinctly heard when all else was quiet, and he had evidently rubbed against some light article of furniture in the outer room and moved it. In the reaction of relief, Cynthia seized Goliath, sat down on the floor, and—cried! having first deposited her candlestick carefully on the table. Joyce did quite the opposite, and laughed hysterically for several minutes. The tension of suspense and terror had been very real.

"How *did* he get in here?" sobbed Cynthia, at length.

"Why, through the window, of course.

And he must have been in before we came.
Don't you remember, we found the door at the
head of the cellar steps open? I closed it
when we came up, so he could n't have got here
afterward." Joyce bent down and scratched
Goliath's fat jowls, at which he purred the
louder.

"Well, let's let him stay, since he's here,"
sighed Cynthia, wiping her eyes. "He'll be
sort of company!" So Goliath was allowed to
remain, and the two girls, escorted by him, proceeded on their voyage of discovery. Back
across the drawing-room and hall they went,
and through the dining-room. There for a
moment they stood, surveying anew the curious scene.

"Does it strike you as strange," Joyce demanded suddenly, "that there's no silver here,
no knives, forks, spoons, sugar-bowls, or—or
anything of that kind? Yet everything else in
china or glass is left. What do you make of
it?"

"Somebody got in and stole it," ventured
Cynthia.

"Nonsense! Nobody's been here since, except ourselves, that's perfectly plain. No, the people must have stopped long enough to collect it and put it away,—or take it with them. Cynthia, why *do* you suppose they left in such a hurry?" But Cynthia, the unimaginative, was equally unable to answer this query satisfactorily, so she only replied:

"I don't know, I'm sure!"

A room, however, beyond the dining-room was awaiting their inspection. In a corner of the latter, two funny little steps led up to a door, and on opening it, they found themselves in the kitchen. This bore signs of as much confusion as the neighboring apartment. Unwashed dishes and cooking utensils lay all about, helter-skelter, some even broken, in the hurry with which they had been handled. But, apart from this further indication of the haste with which a meal had been abandoned unfinished, there was little to hold the interest, and the girls soon turned away.

"Now for up-stairs!" cried Joyce. "That's where I've been longing to get. We will find

something interesting there, I'll warrant."
With Goliath scampering ahead, they climbed
the white, mahogany-railed staircase. On the
upper floor they found a wide hall correspond-
ing with the one below, running from front to
back, crossed by a narrower one connecting the
wings with the main part of the house. Turning to their left, they went down the narrow
one, peering about them eagerly. The doors
of several bedrooms stood open.

Into the first they entered. The high, old-
fashioned, four-post bed with its ruffled valance and tester was still smoothly made up and
undisturbed. The room was in perfect order.
But Joyce's eye was caught by two candlesticks standing on the mantel.

"Here's a find!" she announced. "We'll
take these to use for our candles. They're
nicer and handier than our tin one. We will
keep that for an emergency."

"But ought we disturb them?" questioned
Cynthia.

"Oh, you are *too* particular! What earthly
harm can it do? Here! Take this one and

49

I 'll carry the other. This must have been a guest-room, and no one was occupying it when —it all happened. Let's look in the one across the hall." This one also proved precisely similar, bed untouched and furniture undisturbed. Another, close at hand, had the same appearance. They next ventured down a narrower hall, over what was evidently the kitchen wing. On each side were bedrooms, four in all, with sparse, plain furnishings and cot-beds. Each room presented a tumbled, unkempt appearance.

"I guess these must have been the servants' rooms," remarked Cynthia.

"That's the first right guess you 've made!" retorted Joyce, good-naturedly, as she glanced about. "And they all left in a hurry, too, judging from the way things are strewn about. I wonder—"

"What?" cried Cynthia, impatient at the long pause.

"Oh, nothing much! I just wonder whether they went off of their own accord, or were dismissed. I can't tell. But one thing I can guess pretty plainly—they went right after the dinner-party and did n't stay over another night. 'Cause why? Most of their beds are made, and they left everything in a muss down-stairs. But come along. This is n't particularly interesting. I want to get to the other end of the hall. Something different 's over there!" They turned and retraced their steps, emerging from the servants' quarters and passing again the rooms they had already examined.

On the other side of the main hall they entered an apartment that was not a bedroom, but appeared to have been used as a sitting-room and for sewing. An old-fashioned sewing-table stood near one window. Two chairs and another table were heaped with material and with garments in various stages of completion. An open work-box held dust-covered spools. But still there was nothing special in the room to challenge interest, and Joyce pulled her companion across the hall toward another partially open door.

They had scarcely been in it long enough to

illuminate it with the pale flames of their candles, before they realized that they were very near the heart of the mystery. It was another bedroom, the largest so far, and its aspect was very different from that of the others. The high four-poster was tossed and tumbled, not, however, as if by a night's sleep, but more as if some one had lain upon it just as it was, twisting and turning restlessly. Two trunks stood on the floor, open and partially packed. One seemed to contain household linen, once fine and dainty and white, now yellowed and covered with the dust of years. The other brimmed with clothing, a woman's, all frills and laces and silks; and a great hoopskirt, collapsed, lay on the floor alongside. Neither of the girls could, for the moment, guess what it was, this queer arrangement of wires and tape. But Joyce went over and picked it up, when it fell into shape as she held it at arm's-length. Then they knew.

"I have an idea!" cried Joyce. "This hoopskirt, or crinoline, I think they used to call it, gave it to me. Cynthia, we must be in the room belonging to the lovely lady whose picture hangs in the library."

"How do you know?" queried Cynthia.

"I don't *know,* I just suspect it. But perhaps we will find something that proves it later." She held the candle over one of the trunks and peered in. "Dresses, hats, waists," she enumerated. "Oh, how queer and old-fashioned they all seem!" Suddenly, with a little cry of triumph, she leaned over and partially pulled out an elaborate silk dress.

"Look! look! what did I tell you! Here is the very dress of the picture-lady, this queer, changeable silk, these big sleeves, and the velvet sewed on in a funny criss-cross pattern! *Now* will you believe me?"

Truly, Cynthia could no longer doubt. It was the identical dress, beyond question. The portrait must have been painted when the garment was new. They felt that at last they had taken a long step in the right direction by thus identifying this room as belonging to the lovely lady of the portrait down-stairs. Joy grew so excited that she could hardly contain a "hurrah," and Cynthia was not far behind her in enthusiasm. But the room had further details to be examined.

An open fireplace showed traces of letters having been torn up and burned. Little, half-charred scraps with faint writing still lay scattered on the hearth. On the dressing-table, articles of the toilet were littered about, and a pair of candlesticks were set close to the mirror. (There were, by the way, no traces of *candles* about the house. Mice had doubtless carried off every vestige of such, long since.) A great wardrobe stood in one corner, the open doors of which revealed some garments still hanging on the pegs, woolen dresses mostly, reduced now to little more than rags through the ravages of moths and mice and time. Near the bed stood a pair of dainty, high-heeled satin slippers, forgotten through the years. Everywhere a hasty departure was indicated, so hasty, as Joyce remarked, "that the lady decided probably not to take her trunks, after all, but left, very likely, with only a hand-bag!"

"And now," cried Joyce, the irrepressible,

"we 've seen everything in this room. Let 's hurry to look at the last one on this floor. That 's right over the library, I think, at the end of the hall. We 've discovered a lot here, but I 've a notion that we 'll find the best of all in there!" As they were leaving the room, Goliath, who had curled himself up on a soft rug before the fireplace, rose, stretched himself, yawned widely, and prepared to follow, wherever they led.

"Does n't he seem at home here!" laughed Cynthia. "I hope he will come every time we do. He makes things seem more natural, somehow." They reached the end of the hall, and Joyce fumbled for the handle, this door, contrary to the usual rule, being shut. Then, for the first time in the course of their adventures in the Boarded-up House, they found themselves before an insurmountable barrier.

The door was locked!

CHAPTER V

YES, the door was locked, and there was
no vestige of a key. Joyce was suddenly inspired with, an idea.

"Let's try the keys of the other doors!   I
noticed that they most all had keys in the locks.
Perhaps one will fit this."   They hunted up
several and worked with them all, but not one
made the slightest impression on this obstinate
lock.

"Now isn't this provoking!" exclaimed
Joyce.   "The only room in the house that we
can't get in, and the most interesting of all,
I'm certain! What *shall* we do?" Cynthia
made no reply, but looked at her little silver
watch.

"Do you know that it's quarter-past six?"
she asked quietly.

JOYCE MAKES A NEW DISCOVERY

"Mercy, no! We 've got to go at once then. How the time has gone!" Reluctantly enough they hunted up Goliath, who in thorough boredom had returned to his place on the hearthrug in the big bedroom, gathered together their candles, and found their way to the cellar. Cynthia had thoughtfully requested a tin biscuit-box from the grocer, and in this they packed their candles, thus protecting them against the ravages of mice, and left them in the cellar near the window. Then they clambered out.

"To-morrow 's Saturday," said Joyce. "In the morning we 'll go to the library and look up that book of costumes. After lunch we 'll go back to the B. U. H. and finish exploring. There 's the attic yet, and maybe we can find that key, too!" With a gay good-by they separated each to her home, on opposite sides of the Boarded-up House.

The result of their researches in the library, next morning, was not wholly satisfactory. They found that the most recent fashion of hoop-skirts or crinolines had prevailed all the way from 1840 to 1870, or thereabouts. And while these dates limited, to a certain extent, the time of the mysterious happening, it did not help them very much. They felt that they must look for some more definite clue.

That afternoon they entered the Boarded-up House for the third time. They found Goliath already in the cellar, owing, no doubt, to the fact that Bates's pup was patrolling the front yard. So they invited him to accompany them, an invitation which he accepted with arched back and resounding purr. Deciding to explore the attic first, they found that a door from the upper hall opened on a stairway leading to it.

At any other time, or in any other house, they would have found this attic of absorbing interest. In its dusky corners stood spinning wheels and winding-reels. Decrepit furniture of an ancient date had found a refuge there. Antique hair trunks lined the sides, under the eaves, and quaint garments hung about on pegs. The attic was the only apartment in this strange house that received the light of day, for the two little windows like staring eyes were not boarded up. So dim were they, however, with dirt and cobwebs, that very little daylight filtered through.

But the attic had no great holding interest at present, since it was evident that it contained no clue to help them in the solution of the mystery. And they soon left it, to search anew every room below, in the hope of coming upon the missing key.

"These old-fashioned keys are so immense that it hardly seems possible that any one would carry one off—far," conjectured Joyce. "But why in the world should just that room be locked, anyway? What can be hidden there? I 'm wild,—simply wild with impatience to see it all!"

The search for the key was not exactly systematic. Neither of the girls felt at liberty to open bureau-drawers or pry into closets and trunks. Besides, as Cynthia wisely suggested, it was not likely that any one would lock a door so carefully and then put the key in a drawer or trunk or on a shelf. They would either carry it away with them or lay it down, forgotten, or hide it in some unusual place. If it had been carried away, of course their search was useless. But if it had been thoughtlessly laid aside somewhere, or even hidden away in some obscure corner, there *was* a possibility that they might come upon it.

With this hope in mind, they went from room to room, searching on desks, chairs, and tables, poking into dark corners, peeping into vases and other such receptacles, and feeling about under the furniture; but all to no purpose. They came at last to the great bedroom where were so many signs of agitation and hurried departure, deciding that here would be the most likely field for discovery. Goliath had evidently preceded them, for they found him once more curled up on the soft rug before the fireplace. He seemed to prefer this comfortable spot to all others, but he rose and stretched when the girls came in. Joyce went straight for the chimneyplace.

"I 'm going to poke among these ashes," she announced. "A lot of things seem to have

"Well, what do you suppose that can be?" queried Cynthia

been burned here, mostly old letters. Who knows but what the key may have been thrown in too!" She began to rake the dead ashes, and suddenly a half-burned log fell apart, dropping something through to the bottom with a "chinking" sound.

"Did you hear that?" she whispered. "Something clinked! Ashes or wood won't make that sound. Oh, suppose it is the key!" She raked away again frantically, and hauled out a quantity of charred debris, but nothing even faintly resembling a key. When nothing more remained, she poked the fragments disgustedly, while Cynthia looked on.

"See there!" Cynthia suddenly exclaimed. "It is n't a key, but what 's that round thing?" Joyce had seen it at the same moment and picked it up—a small, elliptical disk so blackened with soot that nothing could be made of it till it was wiped off. When freed from its coating of black, one side proved to be of shining metal, probably gold, and the other of some white or yellowish substance, the girls could not tell just what. In the center of this was a curious smear of various dim colors.

"Well, what do you suppose that can be?" queried Cynthia.

"I can't imagine. Whatever it was, the fire has pretty well finished it. You can see that it must have been rather valuable once,— there's gold on it. Here's another question to add to our catechism: what is it, and why was it thrown in the fire? Whatever it was, it does n't help much now. If it had only been the key!—Good gracious! is that a rat?" Both girls jumped to their feet and stood listening to the strange sounds that came from under the valance hanging about the bottom of the great four-poster bed. It was a curious, intermittent, irregular sound, as of something being pushed about the floor. After they had listened a moment, it suddenly struck them both that the noise was somehow very familiar.

"Why, it's Goliath, of course!" laughed Cynthia. "This is the second time he has scared us. He has something under there that he's playing with, knocking it about, you know. Let's see what it is!" They tiptoed over and raised the valance.

Cynthia was right. Goliath was under the bed, dabbing gracefully with one paw at something attached to a string or narrow ribbon. Despite the rolls of dust that lay about, Joyce crawled under and rescued it. She emerged with a flushed face and a triumphant chuckle. "Goliath beats us all!! He's made the best find yet!"

"Is it the key?" cried Cynthia.

"No, it's this!" And before Cynthia's astonished eyes Joyce dangled a large gold locket, suspended on a narrow black velvet ribbon. In the candle-light the locket glistened with tiny jewels.

"Do you recognize it?" demanded Joyce.

"*Recognize* it? How should I?"

"Why, Cynthia! It's the very one that hangs about the neck of our Lovely Lady in the picture down-stairs!" It was, indeed, no other. Even the narrow black velvet ribbon was identical.

"She must have dropped it accidentally,

perhaps when she took it off, and it rolled under the bed. In her hurry she probably forgot it," said Joyce, laying it beside the curious disk they had raked from the fireplace. "Is n't it a beauty? It must be very valuable." Cynthia bent down and examined both articles closely.

"Did you notice, Joyce," she presently remarked, "that those two things are exactly the same shape, and almost the same size?"

"Why, so they are!" exclaimed Joyce. "Oh, I have an idea, Cynthia! Can we open the locket? Let's try." She picked it up and pried at the catch with her thumb-nail. After a trifling resistance it yielded. The locket fell open and revealed itself—empty. Joyce took up the disk and fitted it into one side. With the gold back pressed inward, it slid into place, leaving no shadow of doubt that it had originally formed part of this trinket.

"Now," announced Joyce, "I know! It was a miniature, an ivory one, but the fire has entirely destroyed the likeness. Question: how came it in the fire?" The two girls stood looking at each other and at the locket, more bewildered than ever by this curious discovery. Goliath, cheated of his plaything, was making futile dabs at the dangling velvet ribbon. Suddenly Joyce straightened up and looked Cynthia squarely in the eyes.

"I 've thought it out," she said quietly. "It just came to me. The miniature was taken out of the locket—on purpose, *to destroy* it! The miniature was of the same person whose picture is turned to the wall down-stairs!"

CHAPTER VI

"CYNTHIA, what's your theory about the mystery of the Boarded-up House?"

The two girls were sitting in a favorite nook of theirs under an old, bent apple-tree in the yard back of the Boarded-up House, on a sunny morning a week later. They were supposed to be "cramming" for the monthly "exams," and had their books spread out all around them. Cynthia looked up with a frown, from an irregular Latin conjugation.

"What's a *theory?*"

"Why, you know! In Conan Doyle's mystery stories *Sherlock Holmes* always has a 'theory' about what has happened, before he really knows; that is, he makes up a story of his own, from the few things he has found out, before he gets at the whole truth."

"Well," replied Cynthia, laying aside her Latin grammar, "since you ask me, my theory is that some one committed a murder in that room we can't get in, then locked it up and went away, and had the house all boarded up so it would n't be discovered. I 've lain awake nights thinking of it. And I 'd just as lief *not* get into that room, if it 's so!"

Joyce broke into a peal of laughter. "Oh, Cynthia! If that is n't exactly like you! Who but you would have thought of such a thing!"

"I don't see anything queer about it," retorted Cynthia. "Does n't everything point that way?"

"Certainly not, Cynthia Sprague! Do you suppose that even years and years ago any one in a big house like this could commit a murder, and then calmly lock up and walk away, and the matter never be investigated? That 's absurd! The murdered person would be missed and people would wonder why the place was left like this, and the—the authorities would get in here in a hurry. No, there was n't any murder or anything bloodthirsty at all; something very different."

"Well, since you don't like *my* theory," replied Cynthia, still nettled, "what's yours? Of course you *have* one!"

"Yes, I have one, and I have lain awake nights, too, thinking it out. I'll tell you what it is, and if you don't agree with me, you're free to say so. Here's the way it all seems to me:

"Whatever happened in that house must have concerned two persons, at least. And one of them, you must admit, was our Lovely Lady whose portrait hangs in the library. Her room and clothes and locket show that. She looks very young, but she must have been some one of importance in the house, probably the mistress, or she would n't have occupied the biggest bedroom and had her picture on the wall. You think that much is all right, don't you?" Cynthia nodded.

"Then there's some one else. That one we don't know anything at all about, but it is n't hard to guess that it was the person whose picture is turned to the wall, and whose miniature was in the locket, and who, probably, occupied the locked-up room. That person must have been some near and dear relation of the Lovely Lady's, surely. But—what? We can't tell yet. It might be mother, father, sister, brother, husband, son, or daughter, any of these.

"The Lovely Lady (I'll have to call her that, because we don't know her name) was giving a party, and every one was at dinner, when word was suddenly brought to her about this relative. Or perhaps the person was right there, and did something that displeased her,—I can't tell which. Whatever it was,—bad news either way,—it could only have been one of two things. Either the relative was dead, or had done something awful and disgraceful. Anyhow, the Lovely Lady was so terribly shocked by it that she dismissed her dinner party right away. I don't suppose she felt it right to do it. It was not very polite, but probably excusable under the circumstances!"

"Maybe she fainted away," suggested Cynthia, practically. "Ladies were always doing that years ago, especially when they heard bad news."

"Good enough!" agreed Joyce. "I never thought of it. She probably did. Of course, that would break up the party at once. Well, when she came to and every one had gone, she was wild, frantic with grief or disappointment or disgust, and decided she just *could n't* stay in that house any longer. She must have dismissed her servants right away, though why she did n't make them clear up first, I can't think. Then she began to pack up to go away, and decided she would n't bother taking most of her things. And sometime, just about then, she probably turned the picture to the wall and took the other one out of her locket and threw it into the fire. Then she went away, and never, never came back any more."

"Yes, but how about the house?" objected Cynthia. "How did that get boarded up?"

"I have thought that out," said Joyce. "She may have stayed long enough to see the boarding up done, or she may have ordered some one to do it later. It can be done from the outside."

"I think she was foolish to leave all her good clothes," commented Cynthia, "and the locket under the bed, too."

"I don't believe she remembered the locket —or cared about it!" mused Joyce. "She was probably too upset and hurried to think of it again. And I 'm sure she lay on the bed and cried a good deal. It looks like that. Now what do you think of my theory, Cynthia?"

"Why, I think it is all right, fine—as far as it goes. I never could have pieced things together in that way. But you have n't thought about who this mysterious relative was, have you?"

"Yes, I have, but, of course, that 's much harder to decide because we have so little to go on. I 'll tell you one thing I 've pretty nearly settled, though. Whatever happened, it was n't that anybody *died!* When people die, you 're terribly grieved and upset, of course, and you *may* shut up your house and never come near it again. I 've heard of such things happening. But you generally put things nicely to rights first, and you don't go away and forget more than half your belongings. If you don't tend to these things yourself, you get some one else to do it for you. And one other thing is certain too. You don't turn the dead relative's picture to the wall or tear it out of your locket and throw it into the fire. You'd be far more likely to keep the picture always near so that you could look at it often. Is n't that so?"

"Of course!" assented Cynthia.

"Then it *must* have been the other thing that happened. Somebody did something wrong, or disappointing, or disgraceful. It must have been a dreadful thing, to make the Lovely Lady desert that house forever. I can't imagine what!"

"But what about the locked-up room?" interrupted Cynthia. "Have you any theory about that? You have n't mentioned it."

"That's something I simply can't puzzle out," confessed Joyce. "The Lovely Lady must have locked it, or the disgraceful relative may have done it, or some one entirely different. I can't make any sense out of it."

"Well, Joy," answered Cynthia, "you 've a theory about what happened, and it certainly sounds sensible. Now, have you any about what relative it was? That 's the next most interesting thing."

"I don't think it could have been her father or mother," replied Joyce, thoughtfully. "Parents are n't liable to cause that kind of trouble, so we 'll count them out. She looks very young, not nearly old enough to have a son or daughter who would do anything very dreadful, so we 'll count *them* out. (Is n't this just like the 'elimination' in algebra!) That leaves only brother, sister, or husband to be thought about."

"You forget aunts, uncles, and cousins!" interposed Cynthia.

"Oh, Cyn! how absurd! They are much too distant. It *must* have been some one nearer than that, to matter so much!"

"I think it 's most likely her husband, then," decided Cynthia. "He 'd matter most of all."

"Yes, I've thought of that, but here's the objection: her husband, supposing she had one, would probably have owned this house. Consequently he would n't be likely to allow it to be shut up forever in this queer way. He'd come back after a while and do what he pleased with it. No, I don't think it was her husband, or that she was married at all. It must have been either a sister or brother,—a younger one probably,—and the Lovely Lady loved her— or him—better than any one else in the world."

"Look here!" interrupted Cynthia, suddenly. "There's the easiest way to decide all this!"

"What is it?" cried Joyce, opening her eyes wide.

"Why, just go in there and turn that picture in the drawing-room around!"

"Oh, Cynthia, you jewel! Of *course* it will be the easiest way! What geese we are to have waited so long! Only it will be a heavy thing to lift. But the time has come when it must be done. Let's go right away!"

Full of new enthusiasm, they scrambled to their feet, approached the cellar window by a

circuitous route (they were always very careful that they should not be observed in this),
and were soon in the dim cellar lighting their
candles. Then they scurried up-stairs, entered the drawing-room, and set their candlesticks on the table. After that they removed
all the breakable ornaments from the mantel and drew another chair close to the fireplace.

"Now," commanded Joyce, stepping on the
seat of one while Cynthia mounted the other,
"be awfully careful. That red silk cord it
hangs by is perfectly rotten. I'm surprised
it hasn't given way before this. Probably, as
soon as we touch the picture the cord will
break. If so, let the picture down gently to
rest on the mantel. Ready!"

They reached out and grasped the heavy
frame. True to Joy's prediction, the silk cord
snapped at once, and the picture's whole weight
rested in their hands.

"Quick!" cried Cynthia. "I can't hold it
any longer!" And with a thud, the heavy bur-
den slipped to the mantel. But there was no

damage done and, feeling on the other side, Joyce discovered that it had no glass.

"Now what?" asked Cynthia.

"We must turn it around as it rests here. We can easily balance it on the mantel." With infinite caution, and some threatened mishaps, they finally got it into position, right side to the front, and sprang down to get their candles. On holding them close, however, the picture was found to be so coated with gray dust that absolutely nothing was distinguishable.

"Get the dust-rag!" ordered Joyce. And Cynthia, all excitement, rushed down cellar to find it. When she returned, they carefully wiped from the painting its inch-thick coating of the dust of years, and again held their candles to illumine the result.

For one long intense moment they stared at it. And then, simultaneously, they broke into a peal of hysterical giggles.

CHAPTER VII

"OH, Cynthia!" gasped Joy at length, "is n't it too comical! We 're just as far from it all as ever!" And they both fell to chuckling again.

They were certainly no nearer the solution of their problem. For, facing the room once more, the mysterious picture looked forth—the portrait of *two babies!* They were plump, placid babies, aged probably about two or three years, and they appeared precisely alike. It took no great stretch of imagination to conjecture what they were—twins—and evidently brother and sister, for one youngster's dress, being a trifle severe in style, indicated that it was doubtless a boy. These two cherubic infants had both big brown eyes, fat red cheeks, and adorable, fluffy golden curls. They were

79

pictured as sitting, hand in hand, on a green bank under a huge spreading tree and gazing solemnly toward a distant church steeple.

"The poor little things!" cried Cynthia. "Think of them having been turned to the wall all these years! Now what was the sense of it,—two innocent babies like that!" But Joyce had not been listening. All at once she put down her candle on the table and faced her companion.

"I 've got it!" she announced. "It came to me all of a sudden. Of course those babies are twins, brother and sister. Any one can tell that! Well, don't you see, one of them—the girl—was our Lovely Lady. The other was her twin brother. It 's all as clear as day! The twin brother did something she did n't like, and she turned his picture to the wall. Hers happened to be in the same frame too, but she evidently did n't care about that. Now what have you to say, Cynthia Sprague?"

"You must be right," admitted Cynthia. "I thought we were 'stumped' again when I first saw that picture, but it 's been of some use,

80

after all. Do you suppose the miniature was a copy of the same thing?"

"It may have been, or perhaps it was just the brother alone when he was older. We can't tell about that." All this while Cynthia had been standing, candle in one hand and dust-cloth in the other. At that point she put the candlestick on the table and stood gazing intently at the dust-cloth. Presently she spoke:

"Joyce, *do* you think there would be any harm in my doing something I 've longed to do ever since we first entered this house?"

"What in the world is that?" queried Joyce.

"Why, I want to *dust* this place, and clear out of the way some of the dirt and cobwebs! They worry me terribly. And, besides, I 'd like to see what this lovely furniture looks like without such quantities of dust all over it."

"Good scheme, Cyn!" cried Joyce, instantly delighted with the new idea. "I 'll tell you what! We 'll come in here this afternoon with old clothes on, and have a regular *house-clean-ing!* It can't hurt anything, I 'm sure, for we

81

won't disturb things at all. I'll bring a dust-cloth, too, and an old broom. But let's go and finish our studying now, and get that out of the way. Hurrah for house-cleaning, this afternoon!"

Filled with fresh enthusiasm, the two girls rushed out to hurry through the necessary studies before the anticipated picnic of the afternoon. If their respective mothers had requested them to perform so arduous a task as this at home, they would, without doubt, have been instantly plunged into deep despair. But because they were to execute the work in an old deserted mansion saturated with mystery, no pleasure they could think of was to be compared with it. This thought, however, did not enter the heads of the enthusiastic pair.

Smuggling the house-cleaning paraphernalia into the cellar window, unobserved, that afternoon, proved no easy task, for Cynthia had added a whisk-broom and dust-pan to the outfit. Joyce came to the fray with an old broom and a dust-cloth, which latter she thought she had carefully concealed under her sweater. But a long end soon worked out and trailed behind her unnoticed, till Goliath, basking on the veranda steps, spied it. The lure proved too much for him, and he came sporting after it, as friskily as a young kitten, much to Cynthia's delight when she caught sight of him.

"Oh, let him come along!" she urged. "I do love to see him about that old house. He makes it sort of cozier. And, besides, he seems to belong to it, anyway. You know he discovered it first!" And so Goliath followed into the Boarded-up House.

They began on the drawing-room. Before they had been at work very long, they found that they had "let themselves in" for a bigger task than they had dreamed. Added to that, performing it by dim candle-light did not lessen its difficulties, but rather increased them tenfold. First they took turns sweeping, as best they could, with a very ancient and frowsy broom, the thick, moth-eaten carpet. When they had gone over it once, and taken up what seemed like a small cart-load of dust, they found that, after all, there remained almost as much as ever on the floor. Cynthia was for going over it again.

"Oh, never mind it!" sighed Joyce. "My arms ache and so do yours. We'll do it again another time. Now let's dust the furniture and pictures." And they fell to work with whisk-broom and dust-cloths. Half an hour later, exhausted and grimy, they dropped into chairs and surveyed the results. It was, of course, as but a drop in the bucket, in comparison with all the scrubbing and cleaning that was needed. Yet, little as it was, it had already made a vast difference in the aspect of the room. Surface dust at least had been removed, and the fine old furniture gave a hint of its real elegance and polish. Joyce glanced at the big hanging candelabrum and sighed with weariness. Then she suddenly remarked:

"Cynthia, we have the *dimmest* light here with only those two candles! Why not have some more burning?"

"We've only three left," commented Cynthia, practical as ever. "And my pocket-

84

money is getting low again, and you have n't any left, as usual. So we 'd better economize till allowance day!"

"Tell you what!" cried Joyce, freshly inspired. "I 've the loveliest idea! Don't you just long to know what this room would look like with that big candelabrum going? I do. They say illumination by candle-light is the prettiest in the world. Sometime I 'm going to buy enough wax candles to fill that whole chandelier—or candelabrum rather—and we 'll light it just once and see how it makes things look. What do you say?"

"It 'll cost you a good deal more than a dollar," remarked Cynthia, after an interval spent in calculation. "Of course I 'd like to see it too, so I 'll go halves with you on the expense. And I don't believe we can get nice *wax* candles, only penny tallow ones. But they 'll have to do. I wonder, though, if people could see the light from the street, through any chinks in the boarding?"

"Of course not," said Joyce. "Don't you see how all the inside shutters are closed and

the velvet curtains drawn? It is n't possible.
Then we 'll have the illumination for a treat,
sometime, and I 'll begin to save up for it.
And I hope before that time we 'll have puzzled out this mystery. I 'm afraid we are n't
very good detectives, or we 'd have done it long
before this. Sherlock Holmes would have!"

"But remember," suggested Cynthia, "that
those Sherlock Holmes mysteries were usually
solved very soon after the thing happened.
This took place years and years ago. I reckon
we 're doing pretty nearly as well as Sherlock,
when you come to think of it."

"Perhaps that 's so," admitted Joyce,
thoughtfully. "It 's not so easy after goodness knows how many years! But I 'm rested
now. Come and see what we can do with the
library. I 'm wild to look at the Lovely Lady
again. I really think I *love* that picture!"
And so, in the adjoining room, they stood a
while with elevated candles, gazing fascinated
at the portrait of the beautiful woman.

"She 's lovely, lovely, lovely!" sighed Joyce.
"Oh, would n't I like to have known her! And

do you notice, Cynthia, she has the same big brown eyes of the girl-baby in the parlor. There is n't a doubt but what that baby was she."

They tore themselves away from the portrait after a time, and commenced digging at the dust and cobwebs of the library. But they were thoroughly tired after their heroic struggles with the drawing-room, and made, on the whole, but little progress. Added to this, their enthusiasm for cleaning-up had waned considerably.

"I guess we 'll have to leave this for another day," groaned Joyce at last. "I 'm just dog-tired!"

"All right," assented Cynthia, in muffled tones, her head being under a great desk in the corner. "But wait till I finish sweeping out under here. *Mercy!* what 's that? I just touched something soft!" On the instant, Joyce was at her side with the candle.

"Why, it 's Goliath as usual!" they both cried, peering in. "Is n't he the greatest for getting into odd corners!" Far at the back sat Goliath, curled into a comfortable ball, his front paws tucked under, and purring loudly.

"He 's sitting on an old newspaper, I think," said Joyce. "He always does that if he can find one, because they 're warm." Suddenly she snatched at the paper so violently that Goliath went tobogganing off with a protesting "meouw."

"Look, look, Cynthia!" she exclaimed, brushing off a cloud of dust with the whiskbroom, and pointing to the top of the sheet. "Here 's one of the biggest discoveries yet!" And Cynthia, following her index-finger, read aloud:

" 'Tuesday, April 16, 1861.' "

"Which proves," added Joyce, "that whatever happened here did n't take place much *earlier* than this date, or the paper would n't be here. What we want to do now is hunt around and see if there are any newspapers of a *later* date. Let 's do it this minute!"

Forgetting all their weariness, they seized their candles and scurried through the house, finding an occasional paper tucked away in some odd corner. But upon examination these all proved to be of earlier date than that of their first discovery. And when it was clear that there were no more to be found, Joyce announced:

"Well, I'm convinced that the Boarded-up House mystery happened not earlier than April 16, 1861, and probably not much later. That's over forty years ago, for this is 1905! Just think, Cynthia, of this place standing shut up and untouched and lonely all that time! It's wonderful!" But Cynthia had turned and snatched up Goliath.

"You precious cat!" she crooned to him as he struggled unappreciatively in her embrace. "You're the best detective of us all! We ought to change your name to 'Sherlock Holmes'!"

CHAPTER VIII

"IT'S no use, Cynthia. We've come to the end of our rope!" Joyce sat back on her heels (she had been rummaging through a box of old trash in the kitchen of the Boarded-up House) and wiped her grimy hands on the dust-cloth. Cynthia, perched gingerly on the edge of a rickety chair, nodded a vigorous assent.

"*I* gave it up long ago. It seemed so hopeless! But you *would* continue to hunt, so I've trotted around after you and said nothing."

More than three weeks had elapsed since the finding of the old newspaper and the definite settling of the date. Filled with new hope over this find, the girls had continued to search diligently through the neglected old mansion, strong in the belief that they would eventually discover, if not the missing key, at least a trail of clues that would lead to the unraveling of the mystery. The mystery, however, refused to be unraveled. They made no further discoveries, and to-day even Joyce expressed herself as completely discouraged.

"There's just one thing that seems to me thoroughly foolish," Cynthia continued. "It's your still insisting that we keep from mentioning the Boarded-up House to outsiders. Good gracious! do you think they're all going to suspect that we're inside here every other day, just because you happen to speak of the place? If you do, it's your guilty conscience troubling you!" Cynthia had never spoken quite so sharply before. Joyce looked up, a little hurt.

"Why, Cynthia, what's the matter with you? One would think I'd been doing something *wrong,* the way you speak!"

"Oh, I did n't mean it that way," explained Cynthia, contritely. "But you don't know how this remembering *not* to speak of it has got on my nerves! I catch myself a dozen times a day just going to make some innocent remark about the B. U. H., generally at the table, and then I stutter and blush, and they all ask what's the matter, and I don't know what in the world to answer! Now I have an idea. Perhaps it isn't worth anything; mine generally aren't! But it's this: why wouldn't it be a good scheme to get the older folks to talk about this house, without letting them know you have any special interest in it—just start the subject, somehow? I notice folks are liable to talk quite a long while on most any subject that's started. And they might have something to say that would interest us, and we *might* get some new clues. And I don't see any reason why they should connect us with it, specially."

Joyce considered the subject in thoughtful silence.

"I believe you're right," she said at last. "It is silly to continue keeping so 'mum' about it, and we might get some good new points. Anyhow, in the detective stories Sherlock Holmes didn't keep everything so quiet, but talked to lots of outside people, and got ideas that way, too. Why did n't I think of it before! Good old Cynthia! You had the right notion that time. Come, let's go home now. I'm tired and sick of this dusty grubbing, and we're not going to do any more of it!"

Next morning, Joyce came flying over to Cynthia's house half an hour before it was time to start for high school. She seemed rather excited.

"Come on! Do hurry, Cyn! I've something important to tell you."

"But it is n't time to start yet," objected Cynthia, "and I'm only half through breakfast. Tell me here!" Joyce gave her a warning glance before turning away.

"Oh, later will do," she remarked casually, and strolled into the sitting-room to chat with Mrs. Sprague. This was sufficient to hasten Cynthia, who usually loved to linger cozily over her morning meal. She had her hat and coat on and her books under her arm inside of seven minutes, and the two girls hurried away together. They were no sooner down the steps than Joyce began:

"Last night an idea came to me, just through some remark that Father happened to make. It's queer we never thought of it before. There's a real-estate agent over the other side of the town—Mr. Wade—and he ought to know everything about all the property here. That's his business. Let's go to his office and ask him about the old house. He doesn't know us, and won't suspect anything. We'll go this afternoon, right after school!"

"But there's a meeting of the Sigma Sigma Society this afternoon," Cynthia remonstrated, "and they're going to give that little play. I'm crazy to see it!"

"I don't care!" cried Joyce, recklessly. "What's the meeting of an old literary society compared to an important thing like this?"

"But we could do it just as well to-morrow."

"I can't wait till to-morrow, Cynthia Sprague!" And that settled the matter.

94

They started on their expedition that very afternoon.

It was a bleak, raw day, and they found Mr. Wade huddled over a red-hot stove in his little office. He stared at them in some surprise as they entered.

"Pardon me," began Joyce, always the spokesman, "but I'd like to ask a question or two about the old boarded-up house on Orchard Avenue." Now the agent was apparently not in the best of spirits that day. Business had been very dull, he had two children at home sick with measles, and he himself was in the first stage of a cold.

"I don't know anything about it!" he mumbled crossly. "It ain't in the market—never was!"

"Oh, we don't want to *buy* it or *rent* it!" explained Joyce, politely. "We only wanted to know if you knew the owners, where they live and what their names are."

"No, I don't!" he reiterated. "Tried to find out once. It's some estate. Business all transacted through lawyers in New York, and they won't open their heads about it. Plain as told me it was none of my affairs!"

"Then perhaps you could tell us—" Joyce was persisting, when the agent suddenly interrupted, turning on her suspiciously:

"Say, what do you want to know all this for? What's the old place to you, anyhow?"

"Oh, nothing—nothing at all!" protested Joyce, alarmed lest their precious secret was about to be discovered. "We only asked out of curiosity. Good day, sir!" And the two girls fled precipitately from the office.

"I was going to ask him the name of the lawyers," Joyce explained as they hurried away. "But it would n't do any good, I guess, if we knew. We could n't go and question *them,* for it's plain from what the agent said that they don't want to talk about it. My, but that man was cranky, was n't he!"

"I think he was sick," said Cynthia. "He looked it. Well, I suppose we will have to give it all up! We 've tried just about everything." Suddenly she stopped and stood perfectly still, staring blankly at nothing.

"Come on!" urged Joyce. "Whatever is the matter with you, standing here like that?"

"I was just thinking—seems to me I remember something about the first day we got into the B. U. H. Did n't you tell me that you knew the house was left furnished, that somebody had told your father so?"

"Why, *of course!*" cried Joyce, excited at once. " I certainly did, and what a stupid I am not to have thought of it since!" And she herself stopped short and stood thinking.

"Well, what is it?" demanded Cynthia, impatiently. "Who's stopping and staring now?"

"The trouble is," said Joyce, slowly, "that the whole thing's not very clear in my mind. It was several years ago that I heard Father mention it. Somebody was visiting us when we first moved here, and asked him at the table about the old house next door. And Father said, I think, that he did n't know anything much about it only that it was a queer old place, and once he had met an elderly lady who

97

happened to mention to him that she knew the house was left furnished, just as it was, and she did n't think the owners would ever live in it again. I don't know why I happened to remember this. It must have made quite an impression on me, because I was a good deal younger and did n't generally listen much to what they were saying at table."

"Well," announced Cynthia, still standing where she had stopped, and speaking with great positiveness, "there 's only one thing to do now, and that is, find out who the old lady is and hunt her up!"

"I suppose I can find out her name from Father—if he remembers it—but what then? I can't go and scrape up an acquaintance with a perfectly strange person, and she *may* live in Timbuctoo!" objected Joyce.

"It 's the only thing left, the 'last resort' as they say in stories," said Cynthia. "But, of course, you can do as you like. You 're engineering this business!"

"Well, I will," conceded Joyce, not very hopefully, however. "I 'll lead Father round

"Do you know any real elderly people, Father!"

to talking of her this evening, if I can, and see what comes of it."

Joyce was as good as her word. That evening when she and her father were seated cozily in the library, she studying, her father smoking and reading his paper, while her mother was temporarily out of the room, she began diplomatically:

"Do you know any real elderly people, Father?" He looked up with a quizzical expression.

"Well, a few. Most people do, don't they? What do you inquire for, Duckie? Thinking of founding an old people's home?" he asked teasingly.

"Oh, no! But who are they, Father? Do you mind telling me?"

"Mercy, Joyce! I can't think just now of all of them!" He was deep in a preëlection article in his paper, and wanted to return to it.

"But can't you think of just a *few?*" she implored.

"Well, you are the queerest child! There's Grandfather Lambert, and your Great-aunt

Lucia, and old Mr. Selby, and—oh, I can't think, Joyce! What's all this foolishness, anyway?" Joyce saw at once that she was getting at nothing very definite along this line, and determined on a bold move.

"Well, who is the old lady that you spoke of once, who, you said, knew something about that queer old boarded-up house next door?"

"Now, why in the world did n't you say so at once, without first making me go through the whole list of my elderly acquaintances?" he laughed. "That was your Great-aunt Lucia."

"*What!*" Joyce almost shouted in her astonishment.

"Why, certainly! What's queer about that? She used to live in New York City, and knew all the best families for miles around. When we first moved here, next to that ramshackle old place, I remember her telling me she 'd known the people who used to live there."

"Who were they?" demanded Joyce, eagerly.

"Oh, I don't remember their name! I

don't know that she ever mentioned it. She only said she knew them, and they'd gone away rather suddenly and left their house all furnished and never came back. Now *do* let me finish my paper in peace, Duckie dear!"

Joyce said no more, and turned again to her studies; but her brain was in a whirl, and she could not concentrate her thoughts on her work. *Great-aunt Lucia!*—of all people! And here she had been wondering how she could ever get to know some stranger well enough to put her questions. But, for that matter, there were difficulties in the way of questioning even Great-aunt Lucia. She was a very old lady, a confirmed invalid, who lived in Poughkeepsie. For many years she had not left her home, and the family seldom saw her; but her father paid a visit to the old lady once in a while when he was in that vicinity.

Joyce then fell to planning how she could get into communication with this Great-aunt Lucia. She couldn't *write* her inquiries,— that certainly would never do! If she could only visit her and get her to talk about it!

But Joyce had never visited this relative in her life, and never particularly wanted to, and it would appear strange to seem suddenly so anxious to see the old lady. This, however, was obviously the only solution, and she began to wonder how it could be arranged. Very prudently, she waited till her father had finished his pipe and laid aside his paper. Then she commenced afresh, but casually, as though the idea had just entered her mind:

"Great-aunt Lucia must be a very interesting old lady, Father!"

"She is, she certainly is! I was always very fond of her. My! how she can talk, and the stories she can tell about old times!" said Mr. Kenway, waxing enthusiastic.

"Oh, I *wish* I could visit her!" exclaimed Joyce.

"Well, you certainly may, if you really want to. I 've always wanted her to see you since you 've grown so, and I 've proposed a number of times that you go with me on the trip. But you 've always refused to be separated from your precious Cynthia, and I could n't think of inflicting *two* youngsters on her." Joyce remembered now, with a good deal of self-reproach, how many times she had begged off from accompanying her father. It had not seemed very interesting then, and, as he had said, she did not want to leave Cynthia, even for two or three days. She realized now that she had not only been a little selfish about it, but had plainly missed a golden opportunity.

"Oh, Father," she cried in real contrition, "I was mean to refuse you! I did n't realize that you *wanted* me to go. I thought you only did it to give me a good time, and, somehow, it did n't seem like a good time—then! When are you going again? And won't you take me?"

"I have n't been there in two years," he mused. "I *ought* to go again soon. The old lady may not live very long, she 's so feeble. Let 's see! Suppose we make it the week-end before election. I 'll write to her to-morrow that we 're all coming, you and Mother and I."

"Oh, but, Father!" exclaimed Joyce.

"Could n't we go sooner? That's nearly a month off!"

"Best I can do, Duckie dear! I simply can't get away before. What's your hurry, anyway? First you won't be hired to go and see her, and then you want to rush off and do it at once! What a funny little daughter it is!" He kissed her laughingly, as she bade him good night.

But Joyce slept little that night. She was wild for morning to come so that she could tell Cynthia, and wilder with impatience to think of the long dragging month ahead before the visit to Great-aunt Lucia, and the solution of the mystery.

CHAPTER IX

THE MEMORIES OF GREAT-AUNT LUCIA

CYNTHIA sat at her desk in high school, alternately staring out of the window, gazing intently across the room at Joyce, and scowling at the blackboard where the cryptic symbols

$$(a + b)^2 = a^2 + 2ab + b^2$$

were being laboriously expounded by the professor of mathematics. Of this exposition, it is safe to say, Cynthia comprehended not a word for the following simple reason. Early that morning Joyce had returned from the visit to her great-aunt Lucia and had entered the class-room late. Cynthia had not yet had a moment in which to speak with her alone. It was now the last period of the day, and her impatience had completely conquered her usual absorbed attention to her studies.

The professor droned on. The class feverishly copied more cryptic symbols in its notebooks. But at last the closing-bell rang, and, after what seemed interminable and totally unnecessary delays, Cynthia found herself out of doors, arm-in-arm with Joyce. Then all she could find to say was:

"Now—*tell me!*" But Joyce was very serious, and very mysterious too.

"Not here," she answered. "I could n't! Wait!"

"Well, where and when, then?" cried Cynthia.

"Home," said Joyce. Then, after a moment,—"No, I 'll tell you in the Boarded-up House! That 's the most appropriate place. We 'll go there straight after we get home." So Cynthia was obliged to repress her impatience a little longer. But at length they had crept through the cellar window, lighted their candles, and were proceeding upstairs.

"Come into the library," said Joyce. "I want to stand right where I can look at the Lovely Lady when I tell you this. It 's all so

strange—so *different* from what we thought!"
So they went through the drawing-room, entered the library, and placed their candlesticks
on the mantel where the light would best illuminate the portrait of the Lovely Lady.
Then Joyce began.

"Great-aunt Lucia is very old and very
feeble. She seemed *so* glad to see us all,—especially me. She talked to me a great deal,
but I did not have a chance to mention this
place to her at all till the last evening we were
there. Mother and Father had gone out to
call on some friends, but it was raining and I
had a sore throat, so they decided not to take
me. I was so glad, because then I could stay
home and talk to Great-aunt Lucia, and it
was the first time I'd been with her long
alone.

"She had been telling me a lot about when
she was a little girl, and asking me about myself. And I had told her about you and how
we'd been together so many years, and what
we did when we weren't in school. And
finally I mentioned, just casually, that we

often played in the grounds of this old house next door and described the place a little to her. Well, that started her, as I was sure it would! She began telling me that it was so strange,—that she had been in this house once, and curiously enough just before it was closed for good. Then, you can warrant, I listened with all my ears!

"She said she had become acquainted with the lady through meeting her a short time before at the house of a friend in New York. This friend had then introduced them,—'Mrs. Hubert Kenway—Mrs. Fairfax Collingwood'!"

"*Mrs.* Collingwood!" cried Cynthia. "And we thought she was n't married!—"

"Well, she was,—and we 've made several mistakes beside that, Cynthia Sprague, as you 'll find out later! It seems that Great-aunt Lucia took quite a fancy to young Mrs. Collingwood. She was so sweet and gracious and charmingly pretty. Later, Great-aunt Lucia discovered that she was a widow, living out here. Her husband had been dead a number of years,—ten, I think. She was a Southerner, having come originally from South Carolina.

"Great-aunt Lucia did not see her again till a few weeks later, when she received an invitation to go with her friend, take luncheon, and spend the day at Mrs. Collingwood's. There were several others invited, about a dozen in all. They all came out by train and drove here in hired carriages from the station, which was a long way off then. It was a beautiful, soft, balmy April day, and spring seemed well begun.

"Great-aunt Lucia said the place was delightful,—an old, Colonial house (it seemed so strange to hear her describe everything just as we 've seen it!). And Mrs. Collingwood was a charming hostess. But they were just finishing luncheon when the strangest thing happened!

"A servant came in and handed Mrs. Collingwood a telegram as she sat at the head of the table. She excused herself to them, tore open the envelope and read it. Then, to their

111

astonishment, she turned first a fiery red, and afterward white as a sheet. Then she sprang to her feet saying, 'Oh!' in a sort of stifled voice. Everyone jumped up too, some so quickly that they knocked over their chairs, and asked if anything dreadful was the matter. Then, all of a sudden, she toppled over and slipped to the floor in a dead faint."

"Did n't I *tell* you so, long ago!" exclaimed Cynthia. "I *said* she probably fainted!"

"Yes, you were right. Well, two or three began to chafe her hands and face, and the rest sent the servants flying for smelling-salts and vinegar. Everything was confusion for a few minutes, till she presently came to. Then they all began again to question her about what was the matter, but she would n't tell them. She just said:

" 'I 've had bad news, dear friends, and it has made me feel quite ill. It is something I cannot speak about. I hope you will not think me thoroughly inhospitable, if I go to my room for a while.' They all told her she must certainly go and lie down, and that they would leave immediately. She begged them not to hurry, but of course they saw that it wasn't best to stay, since she wouldn't let them do anything for her. So, fifteen minutes later they were all driving away in the carriages which had remained for them at the house. And—" here Joyce paused dramatically,—"not one of them, except my great-aunt's friend, Mrs. Durand, ever saw her again!"

"But—but—" began Cynthia.

"Wait," said Joyce. "I haven't finished yet! Of course, all of them were crazy to know what happened, but most of them never did,—not till long, long afterward, anyway. There was one that did know soon, however, and that was Mrs. Durand. Two nights afterward, Mrs. Durand was astounded to have Mrs. Collingwood arrive at her house in New York, and beg to be allowed to stay there a day or two. She was dressed entirely in black, and carried only a small grip. Of course, Mrs. Durand took her right in, and that night Mrs. Collingwood told her what had happened.

"But first, I must tell you that Mrs. Colling-wood had a son—"

"*What?*" gasped Cynthia, staring up at the girlish picture.

"Yes, a son! And not a baby, either, but a fine, handsome young fellow of seventeen. Great-aunt Lucia says that Mrs. Collingwood was married when she was only seventeen, and that she was thirty-five when all this happened. But she looked much younger. So that accounts for our mistake! The son was away at Harvard College,—or at least they *thought* he was, at the time of the luncheon. But Great-aunt Lucia says that the same afternoon, as they were driving to the station, they met a splendid young fellow with yellow hair and bright brown eyes, hurrying along the road in the opposite direction. He took off his cap to them gaily, and Mrs. Durand whispered that it was young Fairfax Collingwood, evidently coming home unexpectedly. Great-aunt Lucia says she will never forget his excited, happy look!

"Now, I'll go back to Mrs. Durand and

114

Mrs. Collingwood. (And all that follows, Mrs. Durand told Great-aunt Lucia long, long long afterward.) Mrs. Collingwood came into the house, and her face looked set like a stone, and she seemed twenty years older than when she was having the luncheon. And Mrs. Durand cried:

" 'Oh, my dear, you have lost some one? You are dressed in mourning!'

" 'Yes,' said Mrs. Collingwood. 'I have lost my son! I am going away.' And Mrs. Durand said:

" 'Oh, how—how sudden! He can't be *dead!* We saw him!' And Mrs. Collingwood answered:

" 'He is dead to me!' And for the longest time, Mrs. Durand could n't get another word from her, except that she had shut up the house and was going home South, to live for good. Well, Mrs. Durand put her right to bed,—she was fairly sick with nervousness and exhaustion. And late that night, she broke down and cried and cried, and told Mrs. Durand everything.

"And, oh, Cynthia! *What* do you think it was? You'd never guess!—You know, the Civil War had just broken out,—Fort Sumter had surrendered and Mrs. Collingwood was a South Carolina woman, and was heart and soul with the Confederacy. She had married a Northern man, and had lived ever since up here, but that did n't make any difference. And all the time war had been threatening, she had been planning to raise a company in South Carolina for her son Fairfax, and put him in command of it. They did those things at that time. Her son did n't know about it, however. She was keeping the news to surprise him.

"And then, that day at luncheon, she received a telegram from him saying he had left college and enlisted—*in the Union army*—and was coming home at once to bid her good-bye before going to the front! The shock of it almost killed her! But later she thought that surely, when he came, she could persuade him out of it.

"And he came that very afternoon. The ladies had met him walking up from the train,

116

She would not tell Mrs. Durand just what happened, but intimated that they had had a dreadful scene. You see, the young fellow had been born and brought up in the North, and *his* sympathies were all with *that* side, and he was just as enthusiastic about it as his mother was about the other. And besides, she 'd never talked to him much about the Southern cause, so he did n't realize how she felt. At last, when he would n't give in, she admitted to Mrs. Durand that she disowned him, and told him never to see her face again.

"When he had gone to his room to pack his things, she went and dismissed her servants, and told them to go at once. Then she locked herself in her room till her boy went away. She never saw him again! After he had gone, that night, she collected all her silver and hid it, and partially packed her own things, and then decided she would n't take them with her. And when she had gone around shutting up the house, it was morning. As soon as it was daylight, she went out and got an old colored carpenter who lived nearby to come and board up the windows and doors. She had the boarding all in the cellar, for it had been made two years before when she went to Europe for six months. It took him nearly all day to finish the work, while she stood around and gave directions. I don't see how she had the strength to do it! When it was all done, she locked the door, walked to the station, took the train for New York, and came to Mrs. Durand." Joyce paused in her recital, from sheer lack of breath, and Cynthia took advantage of the silence.

"So *that* was the way of it! And *we* thought it was her brother, and that he 'd done something awful,—committed a robbery or forged something! I don't see why that young Fairfax should have been treated so! I think what he did was fine!"

"You must remember," said Joyce, "that people felt so differently about such things in those days. We can't quite realize it now, and should n't judge them for the way they acted. I suppose Mrs. Collingwood could have forgiven him more easily if he 'd committed a burglary instead! And Great-aunt Lucia says she was terribly high-tempered, too."

"I *can't* understand it, even so!" insisted Cynthia. "But did your great-aunt say anything about those pictures?"

"No, but I asked her if Mrs. Collingwood had any other children, and she said she understood that Fairfax had been a twin, but his little sister had died when she wasn't much more than three years old. So that's the explanation of the two babies in the other room. I suppose Mrs. Collingwood didn't tell all,— in fact I said she didn't tell any details about what happened that night. Probably she turned the portrait around and tore out the miniature when she was alone. But I haven't finished my story yet!"

"Oh, do go on then!" implored Cynthia.

"Mrs. Collingwood stayed at her friend's house two days," continued Joyce, "and then left for her old home in a little town in South Carolina and never came North again. Mrs. Durand never saw her again, either, but used to hear from her at very long intervals. But here's where the awful thing comes in. After the battle of Shiloh, a year later, when the papers published the list of killed—Fairfax Collingwood's name was among the first! So he did not live very long, you see. But what a terrible thing for the poor mother to think that she and her son had parted in anger, and now were never, never to meet again, and make it all up! Oh, I can hardly bear to think of it!" Joyce's eyes were full of tears, as she gazed up at the proud, beautiful face above them.

"Well, that's the end of the story, and that's the tragedy and mystery about this Boarded-up House. Oh!—there's one other thing,—Great-aunt Lucia says she thinks Mrs. Collingwood is still alive,—a very old lady, living down in the little old South Carolina town of Chesterton. She will never allow this old house to be touched nor let any one enter it. But she has made a will, leaving it to the Southern Society when she dies. That's positively all, and you see everything is explained."

"No, it is n't!" retorted Cynthia. "You have n't explained *one* thing, at all!"

"What 's that?" asked Joyce.

"The mystery of the locked-up room!" replied Cynthia.

CHAPTER X

AN EXCITING DISCOVERY

THE autumn of that year ended, the winter months came and went with all their holiday festivities, and spring entered in her appointed time. The passing winter had been filled with such varied outside activities for the two girls, that there was little time to think of the Boarded-up House, and still less to do any further investigating within it. Added to that, the cold had been so constant and intense that it would have been unsafe to venture into the unlighted, unheated, and unventilated old mansion.

But, in spite of these things, its haunting story was never out of their minds for long, and they discussed and re-discussed it in many a spare hour when they crouched cozily by themselves over the open fire during that long winter. It was a wonderful and appealing secret that they somehow felt was all their own. It was better, more interesting than the most engrossing story they had ever read. And the fascination of it was that, though they now knew so much, they did not yet know all. The mystery of the locked room always confronted them, always lured them on!

Once, on a day that was unusually mild, they ventured into the old house for a few moments, and looked long and intently at the Lovely Lady over the library mantel, and at the two pretty children in the drawing-room.

"Yes, that is the boy," said Cynthia. "You can see, even there, what a fine young fellow he must have made, with those big brown eyes and that curly golden hair. Oh, the poor mother!—How she must have grieved, all these years! You can see that she has never gotten over it, or she would have come back here sometime. I wonder if she is alive yet!"

In the library, Joyce picked up the paper that had been discovered through the help of Goliath, and looked it over curiously.

"Why in the world did n't we *read* this paper when we found it!" she exclaimed disgustedly. "Just see here,—the big headlines,— 'Fort Sumter Surrenders. War Formally Declared. Troops Rushing To Washington!' Why, Cynthia, it would surely have given us the clue!"

"I don't think it would have," declared Cynthia, sceptically. "I never would have connected anything in the paper with what happened here."

"Sherlock Holmes would have," mused Joyce. "Well, anyway, we got at the story in another fashion. But oh, Cynthia, will we ever know about the locked-up room?" As Cynthia could cast no further light on this vexed question, they were forced to drop it.

Then came spring, and the ancient cherry-trees in the enclosure back of the Boarded-up House blossomed anew. One brilliant Saturday morning early in May, the girls clambered through the fence with their books and fancy-work, to spend some of the shining hour under the white canopy of blossoms. They were

"Oh, I *wish* I were Sherlock Holmes!"

reading aloud the "Sign of Four," (they inclined much toward mystery and detective stories at this time) turn and turn about, while the one who did not have the book sewed or embroidered. Presently Joyce laid down the volume with a big sigh.

"Oh, I *wish* I were Sherlock Holmes!"

"Mercy! what for?" cried Cynthia. "I 'm sure *I* don't!"

"Why, do you suppose Sherlock would have been all this time getting at the final facts about our Boarded-up House? Of course not! He 'd have had it all worked out and proved by now!" Joyce got to her feet and began roaming about restlessly. Suddenly she stopped in front of her companion.

"I tell you, Cynthia, it *haunts* me! I can't explain to you why, but I feel there is something we have n't discovered yet,—something we *ought* to know. It is n't just 'idle curiosity' as Professor Marlow would call it! I never knew or heard of anything that went so —so *deep* in me as this thing has. That poor, loving, proud mother, and her terrible misunderstanding with her splendid son!—He was *right*, too, I can't help but think. But was she in the wrong? I suppose we can't judge about how people felt in those days. The whole thing is so different now,—all forgotten and forgiven! But I 've read that the Confederates considered their cause almost a—a *religion*. So of course she would have felt the shock of what her son did, terribly. And think how he must have felt, too!

"And then to lose his life, almost in the beginning! Perhaps he and his mother might have made it all up after the war was over, if he 'd only lived. It 's—it 's the saddest thing I ever heard!" Cynthia had risen too, and they linked arms, strolling up and down the little orchard as they talked.

"I feel exactly as you do about it, though I don't often speak of it," said Cynthia. "But, by the way, did it ever strike you that we might find it interesting to look over some of the books in that old library? Some of them looked very attractive to me. And even if it did n't lead to anything, at least it would be good fun to examine them. I love old books! Why not do it this afternoon?"

"Just the thing!" agreed Joyce. "I 've thought of that too, but we 've never had much chance to do it, till now. This afternoon, right after lunch!"

So the afternoon found them again in the dim, musty old library, illuminating the scene extravagantly with five candles. Three sides of the room were lined with bookshelves, reaching nearly to the ceiling. The girls surveyed the bewildering rows of books, puzzled where to begin.

"Oh, come over here!" decided Joyce, choosing the side opposite the fireplace. "These big volumes look so interesting." She brushed the thick dust off their backs, revealing the titles. "Look!—They 're all alike, with red backs and mottled sides." She opened one curiously. "Why!—they 're called 'Punch'! What a strange name! What kind of books can they be?" And then, on further examination,— "Oh! I see. It 's a collection of English papers full of jokes and politics and that sort of thing. And this one is from way back in 1850. Why, Cynthia, these are the most *interesting* things!—"

But Cynthia had already extracted another volume and was absorbed in it, chuckling softly over the old-time humor. Joyce grouped the five candles on the floor and they sat down beside them, from time to time pulling out fresh volumes, reading aloud clever jokes to each other, and enjoying themselves immensely, utterly unconscious of the passing moments.

At length they found they had skimmed through all the volumes of "Punch," the last of which was dated 1860, and had them piled up on the floor beside them. This left a long space on the shelf from which they came, and the methodical Cynthia presently rose to put them back. As she fitted in the first volume, her eye was suddenly caught by something back of the shelves, illuminated in the flickering candle-light.

"Joyce, come here!" she called in a voice of suppressed excitement. And Joyce, who had wandered to another corner, came over in a hurry.

"What is it?"

"Look in there!" Joyce snatched a candle and held it close to the opening made by the books. Then she gave a long, low whistle.

"What do you make of it?" demanded Cynthia.

"Just what it is! And that's as 'plain as a pikestaff'—a *keyhole!*" Cynthia nodded.

"Yes, but what a strange place for it—back of those shelves!—" They brought another candle and examined the wall back of the shelves more carefully. There was certainly a keyhole—a rather small one—and around it what appeared to be the paneling of a door, only partially visible through the shreds of old, torn wall-paper that had once covered it.

"I have it!" cried Joyce, at length. "At least, I think this may be an explanation. That's a small door, without a doubt,—perhaps to some unused closet. Maybe there was a time, when this house was new, when this room was n't a library. Then somebody wanted to make it into a library, and fill all this side of the room with book-shelves. But that door was in the way. So they had it all papered over, and just put the shelves in front of it, as though it had never been there. You see the paper has fallen away, probably through dampness,—and the mice seem to have eaten it too. And here's the keyhole! Is n't it *lucky* we just happened to take the books out that were in front of it!"

"But what are we going to do about it?" questioned Cynthia.

"Do? Why, there's just one thing to do, and that is move the shelves out somehow,— they seem to be movable, just resting on those end-supports,—and get at that door!"

"But suppose it's locked?"

"We'll have to take a chance on that! Come on! We can't move these books and shelves away fast enough to suit me!"

They fell to work with a zest the like of which they had not known since their first entrance into the Boarded-up House. It was no easy task to remove the armfuls of books necessary to get at the door behind, and then push and shove and struggle with the dusty shelves. In a comparatively short time, however, the floor behind them was littered with volumes hastily deposited, and the shelves for a space nearly as high as their heads were removed. Then they tore at the mouldy shreds of wallpaper till the entire frame of the paneled wooden doorway was free. Handle there was none, it having doubtless been removed when the place was papered. There seemed, consequently, no way to open the door. But Cynthia was equal to this emergency.

"I 've seen an old chisel in the kitchen. We might pry it open with that," she suggested.

"Go and get it!" commanded Joyce, bursting with excitement. "I think this is going to be either a secret cupboard or room!"

Cynthia seized a candle and hurried away, coming back breathless with the rusty tool.

"Now for it!" muttered Joyce. She grasped the chisel and inserted it in the crack, pushing on it with all her might. But the door resisted, and Cynthia was just uttering the despairing cry,—

"Oh, it's locked too!" when it suddenly gave way, with a wholly unexpected jerk, and flew open emitting a cloud of dust.

"Mercy!" exclaimed Joyce, between two sneezes, "That almost knocked me off my feet. Did you ever see so much dust!" Snatching the candles again, they both sprang forward, expecting to gaze into the dusty interior of some long unused cupboard or closet. They had no sooner put their heads into the opening, than they started back with a simultaneous cry.

The door opened on a tiny, narrow stairway, ascending into the dimness above!

CHAPTER XI

THE ROOM THAT WAS LOCKED

BEFORE Cynthia could realize what had happened or was happening, Joyce seized her and began waltzing madly around the library, alternately laughing, sobbing, hugging, and shaking her distractedly.

"Stop, stop, Joyce! *Please!*" she begged breathlessly. "Have you gone crazy? You act so! What *is* the matter?"

"*Matter!*—You ask me *that?*" panted Joyce. "You great big *stupid!*—Why, we 've discovered the way to the locked-up room!—That 's what 's the matter!" Cynthia looked incredulous.

"Why, certainly!" continued Joyce. "Can't you *see?* You know that room is right over this. Where else could those stairs lead, then? But come along! We 'll settle all doubts in a moment!" She snatched up a candle again and led the way, Cynthia following without more ado.

"Oh, Joyce! It's horribly dirty and stuffy and cobwebby in here! Could n't we wait a few moments till some air gets in?" implored Cynthia in a muffled voice.

"I sha'n't wait a moment, but you may if you wish," called back Joyce. "But I know you won't! Mind your head! These are the tiniest, lowest stairs I 've ever seen!" They continued to crawl slowly up, their candles flickering low in the impoverished air of the long-inclosed place.

"What if we can't open the door at the top?" conjectured Cynthia. "What if it 's behind some heavy piece of furniture?"

"We 'll just *have* to get in somehow!" responded Joyce. "I 've gone so far now, that I believe I 'd be willing to break things open with a charge of dynamite, if we could n't get in any other way! Here I am, at the top. Now you hold my candle, and we 'll see what happens!" She handed her candle to Cynthia, braced herself, and threw her whole weight against the low door, which was knobless like the one below.

Then came the surprise. She had expected resistance, and prepared to cope with it. To her utter amazement, there was a ripping, tearing sound, and she found herself suddenly prone upon the floor of the most mysterious room in the house! The reason for this being that the door at the top was covered on the inner side with only a layer or two of wallpaper, and no article of furniture happened to stand in front of it. Consequently it had yielded with ease at the tremendous shove Joyce had given it, and she found herself thus forcibly and ignominiously propelled into the apartment.

"My!" she gasped, sitting up and dusting her hands, "but that was sudden! I don't care, though! I'm not a bit hurt, and—we're *in!*" They were indeed "in"! The mysterious, locked room was at last to yield up its secret to them. They experienced a delicious thrill of expectation, as, with their candles raised above their heads, they peered eagerly about.

Now, what they had expected to find within that mysterious room, they could not perhaps have explained with any definiteness. Once they stood within the threshold, however, they became slowly conscious of a vague disappointment. Here was nothing so very strange, after all! The room appeared to be in considerable disorder, and articles of clothing, books, and boyish belongings were tossed about, as in a hurry of packing. But beyond this, there was nothing much out of the ordinary about it.

"Well," breathed Cynthia at length. "Is *this* what we've been making all the fuss about!"

"Wait!" said Joyce. "You can't see everything just at one glance. Let's look about a little. Oh, what a dreadful hole we've made in the wall-paper! Well, it can't be helped now, and it's the only damage we've done." They commenced to tiptoe about the room, glancing curiously at its contents.

THE ROOM THAT WAS LOCKED

It was plainly a boy's room. A pair of fencing-foils hung crossed on one wall, a couple of boxing-gloves on another. College trophies decorated the mantel. On a center-table stood a photograph or daguerreotype in a large oval frame. When Cynthia had wiped away the veil of dust that covered it, with the dust-cloth she had thoughtfully tucked in her belt, the girls bent over it.

"Oh, Cynthia!" cried Joyce. "Here they are—the Lovely Lady and her boy. He must have been about twelve then. What funny clothes he wore! But isn't he handsome! And see how proudly she looks at him. Cynthia, how *could* he bear to leave this behind! I shouldn't have thought he'd ever want to part with it."

"Probably he went in such a hurry that he couldn't think of everything, and left this by mistake. Or he may even have had another copy," Cynthia added in a practical afterthought.

Garments of many descriptions, and all of old-time cut, were flung across the bed, and on the floor near it lay an open valise, half packed with books.

"He had to leave that too, you see, or perhaps he intended to send for it later," commented Joyce. "Possibly he did n't realize that his mother was going to shut up the house and leave it forever. Here 's his big, business-like-looking desk, and in pretty good order, too. I suppose he had n't used it much, as he was so little at home. It 's open, though." She began to dust the top, where a row of school-books were arranged, and presently came to the writing-tablet, which she was about to polish off conscientiously. Suddenly she paused, stared, rubbed at something with her duster, and bending close, stared again. In a moment she raised her head and called in a low voice:

"Cynthia, come here!" Cynthia, who had been carefully dusting the college trophies on the mantel, hurried to her side.

"What is it? What have you found?" Joyce only pointed to a large sheet of paper lying on the blotter. It was yellow with age

140

and covered with writing in faded ink,—writing in a big, round, boyish hand. It began,—

"My dearest Mother—" Cynthia drew back with a jerk, scrupulously honorable, as usual. "Ought we to read it, Joyce? It's a letter!"

"I did," whispered Joyce. "I could n't help it, for I did n't realize what it was at first. I don't think it will harm. Oh, Cynthia, *read* it!" And Cynthia, doubting no longer, read aloud:

My dearest Mother,—the best and loveliest thing in my life,—I leave this last appeal here, in the hope that you will see it later, read it, and forgive me. We have had bitter words, but I am leaving you with no anger in my heart, and nothing but love. That we shall not see each other again in this life, I feel certain. Therefore I want you to know that, to my last hour, I shall love you truly, devotedly. I am so sure I am right, and I have pledged my word. I cannot take back my promise. I never dreamed that you feel as you do about this cause. My mother, my own mother, forgive me, and God keep you.

Your son,

Fairfax.

When Cynthia had ended, there was a big lump in Joyce's throat, and Cynthia herself coughed and flourished a handkerchief about her face with suspicious ostentation. Suddenly she burst out:

"I think that woman must have had a—a heart of *stone,* to be so unforgiving to her son, —after reading this!"

"She never saw it!" announced Joyce, with a positiveness that made Cynthia stare.

"Well!—I'd like to know how you can say a thing like that!" Cynthia demanded at once. "It lay right there for her to see!"

"How do you account for this room being locked?" parried Joyce, answering the question, Yankee fashion, by asking another. Cynthia pondered a moment.

"I *don't* account for it! But—why, of course! The boy locked it after him when he went away, and took the key with him!" Joyce regarded her with scorn.

"That *would* be a sensible thing to do, now, wouldn't it! He writes a note that he is hoping with all his heart that his mother will see.

Then he calmly locks the door and walks off with the key! What for?"

"If he didn't do it, who did?" Cynthia defended herself. "Not the servants. They went before he did, probably. There's only one person left—his mother!"

"You've struck it at last. What a good guesser you are!" said Joyce, witheringly. Then she relented. "Yes, she must have done it, Cynthia. She locked the door, and took the key away, or did something with it,—though what on earth *for,* I can't imagine!"

"But what makes you think she did it *before* she read the note?" demanded Cynthia.

"There are just two reasons, Cynthia. She couldn't have been *human* if she'd read that heart-rending letter and not gone to work at once and made every effort to reach her son! But there's one other thing that makes me *sure.* Do you see anything *different* about this room?" Cynthia gazed about her critically. Then she replied:

"Why, no. I can't seem to see anything so

different. Perhaps I don't know what you mean."

"Then I 'll tell you. Look at the windows! Are they like the ones in the rest of the house?"

"Oh, no!" cried Cynthia. "Now I see! The curtains are not drawn, or the shutters closed. It 's just dark because it 's boarded up outside."

"That 's precisely it!" announced Joyce. "You see, she must have gone around closing all the other inside shutters tight. But she never touched them in this room. Therefore she probably never came in here. The desk is right by the window. She could n't have helped seeing the letter if she had come in. No, for some reason we can't guess, she locked the door,—and never knew!"

"And she never, never will know," whispered Cynthia. "That 's the saddest part of it!"

CHAPTER XII

THE Friday afternoon meeting of the Sigma Sigma literary society broke up with the usual confused mingling of chatter and laughter. There had been a lively debate, and Joyce and Cynthia, as two of the opponents, had just finished roundly and wordily belaboring each other. They entwined arms now, amiably enough, and strolled away to collect their books and leave for home. Out on the street, Cynthia suddenly began:

"Do you know, we 've never had that illumination in the Boarded-up House that we planned last fall, when we commenced cleaning up there."

"We never had enough money for candles," replied Joyce.

"Yes, I know. But still I 've always

145

wanted to do it. Suppose we buy some and try it soon,—say to-morrow?" Joyce turned to her companion with an astonished stare.

"Why, Cynthia Sprague! You *know* it's near the end of the month, and I'm down to fifteen cents again, and I guess you aren't much better off! What nonsense!"

"I have two dollars and a half. I've been saving it up ever so long—not for that specially—but I'm perfectly willing to use it for that."

"Well, you are the queerest one!" exclaimed Joyce. "Who would have thought you'd care so much about it! Of course, I'm willing to go in for it, but I can't give my share till after the first of the month. Why do you want to do it so soon?"

"Oh, I don't know—just because I *do!*" replied Cynthia, a little confused in manner. "Come! Let's buy the candles right off. And suppose we do a little dusting and cleaning up in the morning, and fix the candles in the candelabrum, and in the afternoon light them up and have the fun of watching them?"

A SLIGHT DISAGREEMENT

Joyce agreed to this heartily, and they turned into a store to purchase the candles. Much to Joyce's amazement, Cynthia insisted on investing in the best *wax* ones she could obtain, though they cost nearly five cents apiece.

"Tallow ones will do!" whispered Joyce, aghast at such extravagance. But Cynthia shook her head, and came away with more than fifty.

"I wanted them *good!*" she said, and Joyce could not budge her from this position. Then, to change the subject, which was plainly becoming embarrassing to her, Cynthia abruptly remarked:

"Don't forget, Joyce, that you are coming over to my house to dinner, and this evening we'll do our studying, so that to-morrow we can have the whole day free. And bring your music over, too. Perhaps we'll have time to practise that duet afterward."

"I will," agreed Joyce, and she turned in at her own gate.

Joyce came over that evening, bringing her books and music. As Mr. and Mrs. Sprague were occupying the sitting-room, the two girls decided to work in the dining-room, and accordingly spread out their books and papers all over the big round table. Cynthia settled down methodically and studiously, as was her wont. But Joyce happened to be in one of her "fly-away humors" (so Cynthia always called them), when she found it quite impossible to concentrate her thoughts or give her serious attention to anything. These moods were always particularly irritating to Cynthia, who rarely indulged in causeless hilarity, especially at study periods. Prudently, however, she made no remarks.

"Let's commence with geometry," she suggested, opening the text-book. "Here we are, at Proposition XVI."

"All right," assented Joyce, with deceptive sweetness. "Give me a pencil and paper, please." Cynthia handed them to her and began:

"Angle A equals angle B."

"*Angel* A equals *angel* B," murmured Joyce after her.

A SLIGHT DISAGREEMENT

"Joyce, I wish you would *not* say that!" interrupted Cynthia, sharply.

"Why not?" inquired Joyce with pretended surprise, at the same time decorating the corners of her diagram with cherubic heads and wings.

"Because it confuses me so I can't think!" said Cynthia. "Please call things by their right names."

"But it makes no difference with the proof, what you call things in geometry," argued Joyce, "whether it's angles or angels or caterpillars or coal-scuttles,—it's all the same in the end!" Cynthia ignored this, swallowed her rising wrath, and doggedly began anew:

"Angle A equals angle B!" But Joyce, who was a born tease, could no more resist the temptation of baiting Cynthia, than she could have refused a chocolate ice-cream soda, so she continued to make foolish and irrelevant comments on every geometrical statement, until, in sheer exasperation, Cynthia threw the book aside.

"It's no use!" she groaned. "You're not

in a studying frame of mind, Joyce—certainly not for geometry. I'll go over that myself Monday morning; but what *you're* going to do about it, I don't know—and I don't much care! But we've got to get through somehow. Let's try the algebra. You always like that. Do you think you could put your mind on it?"

"I'll try," grinned Joyce, in feigned contrition. "I'll make the greatest effort. But you don't seem to realize that I'm actually working *very* hard to-night!" Cynthia opened her algebra, picked out the problem, and read:

"'A farmer sold 300 acres—'" when Joyce suddenly interrupted:

"Do you know, Cynthia, I heard the most interesting problem the other day. I wonder if you could solve it."

"What is it?" asked Cynthia, thankful for any awakening symptom of interest in her difficult friend.

"Why, this," repeated Joyce with great gravity. "'If it takes an elephant ten minutes to put on a white vest, how many pan-

cakes will it take to shingle a freight-car?'"
Cynthia's indignation was rapidly waxing hotter, but she made one more tremendous effort to control it.

"Joyce, I told you that I was serious about this studying."

"But so am I!" insisted the wicked Joyce. "Now let's try to work that out. Let x equal the number of pancakes—" The end of Cynthia's patience had come, however. She pushed the books aside.

"Joyce Kenway, you are—*abominable!* I wish you would go home!"

"Well, I won't!" retorted Joyce, giggling inwardly, "but I'll leave you to your own devices, if you like!" And she rose from the table, walked with great dignity to a distant rocking-chair, seated herself in it, and pretended to read the daily paper which she had removed from its seat. From time to time she glanced covertly in Cynthia's direction. But there was no sign of relenting in that young lady. She was, indeed, too deeply indignant, and, moreover, had immersed herself in her work. Presently Joyce gave up trying to attract her attention, and began to read the paper in real earnest,—a thing which she seldom had the time or the interest to do.

There was a long silence in the room, broken only by the scratch of Cynthia's pencil or the rustling of a turned page. Suddenly Joyce looked up.

"Cynthia!" she began. Her voice sounded different now. It had lost its teasing tone and seemed a little muffled. But Cynthia was obdurate.

"I don't want to talk to you!" she reiterated. "I wish you 'd go home!"

"Very well, Cynthia, I will!" answered Joyce, quietly. And she gathered up her books and belongings, giving her friend a queer look as she left the room without another word.

Later, Cynthia put away her work, yawned, and rose from the table. She was beginning to feel just a trifle sorry that she had been so short with her beloved friend.

"But Joyce was simply impossible, tonight!" she mused. "I never knew her to be quite so foolish. Hope she is n't really offended. But she 'll have forgotten all about it by to-morrow morning. . . . I wonder where to-day's paper is? Joyce was reading it—or pretending to! I want to see the weather report for to-morrow. I hope it 's going to be fair. . . . Pshaw! I can't find it. She must have gathered it up with her things and taken it with her. That was mighty careless—but just like Joyce! I 'm going to bed!"

CHAPTER XIII

THE GREAT ILLUMINATION

THE next morning the two girls met, as though absolutely nothing unpleasant had happened. These little differences were, as a fact, of frequent occurrence, and neither of them ever cherished the least grudge toward the other when they were over. Not a word was said in reference to it by either, but Cynthia noticed Joyce looking at her rather curiously several times. Finally she asked:

"What are you staring at me so for, Joyce?"

"Oh, nothing! I was n't staring," Joyce replied, and began to talk of something else.

"By the way, Cyn, why would n't it be a good idea to wait till next week before we have our illumination? Perhaps we could get more candles by that time, too. I vote for next Saturday instead of to-day."

THE GREAT ILLUMINATION

"I can't see why you want to wait," replied Cynthia. "To-day is just as good a time as any. In fact, I think it's better. Something might happen that would entirely prevent it next week. No, let's have it to-day. My heart is set on it."

"Very well then," assented Joyce. "But, do you know, I believe, if this time is a success, we might have it again next Saturday, too."

"Well, you can have it if you like, and if you can raise the money for candles," laughed Cynthia; "but you mustn't depend on me. I'll be 'cleaned out' by that time!"

That morning they carefully dusted the drawing-room and library of the Boarded-up House.

"We'll put the candles in the drawing-room, in the big candelabrum. That will take about forty—and we'll have enough for the library too," said Cynthia, planning the campaign. "And the rest of the candles we'll put in the 'locked-up room.' Let's go right up there now and dust it!"

"Oh, what do you want to light *that* room

for!" cried Joyce. "Don't let's go in there. It makes me blue—even to think of it!" But Cynthia was obdurate.

"I want it lit up!" she announced. "If you don't feel like going up, I'll go myself. I don't mind. But I want candles there!"

"Oh, if you insist, of course I'll go! But really, Cynthia, I don't quite understand you to-day. You want to do such queer things!"

"I don't see anything *queer* about that!" retorted Cynthia, blushing hotly. "It just seemed—somehow—appropriate!"

But Joyce, in spite of her protests, accompanied Cynthia up the tiny, cramped stairway, the entrance to which they had not blocked by restoring the book-shelves.

"What a strange thing it is,—this secret stairway!" she marveled aloud. "I'm sure it *is* a secret stairway, and that it was long unused, even before Mrs. Collingwood left here. I even feel pretty certain that she never knew it was here."

"How do you figure that out?" questioned Cynthia.

"Well, in several ways. For one thing, because it was all closed up and papered over. That could have been done before she came here, and you know she only lived in this house eighteen years. But mainly because there would n't have been much sense in her locking up the room (if she *did* lock it) had she known there was another easy way of getting into it. No, I somehow don't think she knew!"

They did their dusting in the locked-up room, and tried to make it look as ship-shape as possible, carefully avoiding, however, the vicinity of the desk. Cynthia arranged six candles in holders, ready to light, and they went down stairs again to arrange the others,— a task that was accomplished with some difficulty, as the candelabrum was rather high, and they were obliged to stand on chairs. At last all was ready and they hurried home to luncheon, agreeing to meet at two for the "great illumination"!

When they returned that afternoon, Cynthia had smuggled over the gas-lighter, which they found a boon indeed in lighting so many candles at such a height. When every tongue of flame was sparkling softly, the girls stepped back to admire the result.

"Isn't it the prettiest thing you ever saw?" cried Joyce in an ecstasy of admiration. "It beats a Christmas-tree all hollow! I've always heard that candle-light was the loveliest of all artificial illumination, and now I believe it. Just see how this room is positively transformed! We never *saw* those pictures properly before."

"Now it looks as it did fifty years ago," said Cynthia, softly. "Of course, houses *were* lighted by gas then, but only city ones or those near the city. I know, because I've been asking about it. Other people had to use horrid oil-lamps. But there were *some* who kept on having candles because they preferred that kind of light—especially in country-houses. And evidently this was one of them."

Joyce eyed her curiously.

"You've certainly been interested in the question of illumination, half a century ago,— but *why*, Cynthia? I never knew you to go so

deeply into anything of this kind before!"
Cynthia started, and blushed again.

"Do you think so," she stammered. "Oh,
well!—it's only because this—this house has
taken hold of me—somehow. I can't get it
out of my mind, day or night!"

"Yes," cried Joyce, "and I remember the
day when I could hardly induce you to enter it!
I just had to *pull* you in, and you disputed
every inch of the way!"

"That's the way with me," returned Cynthia. "I'm not quick about going into things,
but once I'm *in,* you can't get me out! And
nothing I ever knew of has made me feel as this
house has. Now I'm going to light the candles in the locked-up room."

"That's the one thing *I* can't understand!"
protested Joyce, as they climbed the tiny stairs
once more. "You seem perfectly crazy about
that room, and it makes me so—so *depressed*
that I hate to go near it! I like the library
and the picture of the Lovely Lady best."

Cynthia did not reply to this but lit the candles and gave a last look about. Then they

returned to the drawing-room. As there was nothing further to do but sit and enjoy the spectacle, the two girls cuddled down on a roomy old couch or sofa, and watched with all the fascination that one watches the soft illumination of a Christmas-tree. Sometimes they talked in low voices, commenting on the scene, then they would be silent for a long period, simply drinking it in and trying to photograph it forever on their memories. Joyce frankly and openly enjoyed it all, but Cynthia seemed nervous and restless. She began at length to wriggle about, got up twice and walked around restlessly, and looked at her watch again and again.

"I wonder how long these candles will last?" questioned Joyce, glancing at her own time-piece. "They are n't a third gone yet. Oh, I could sit here and look at this for hours! It's all so different from anything we 've ever seen."

"*What 's that!*" exclaimed Cynthia, suddenly and Joyce straightened up to listen more intently.

There was nothing to do but sit and enjoy the spectacle

THE GREAT ILLUMINATION

"I don't hear anything. What *is* the matter with you to-day, Cynthia Sprague?"

"I don't know. I 'm nervous, I guess!"

"There—I *did* hear something!" It was Joyce who spoke. "The queerest *click!* Good gracious, Cynthia! Just suppose somebody should take it into his head to get in here to-day! Of *all* times! And find this going on!" But Cynthia was not listening to Joyce. She was straining her ears in another direction.

"There it is again! Somebody is at that front door!" cried Joyce. "I believe they must have seen these lights through some chink in the boarding and are breaking in to find out what 's the matter! Perhaps they think—"

Cr-r-r-rack!—Something gave with a long, resounding noise, and the two girls clasped each other in an agony of terror. It came from the front door, there was no shadow of doubt, and somebody had just succeeded in opening the little door in the boarding. There was still the big main door to pass.

"Come!—quick!—quick!" whispered Joyce. "It will *never* do for us to be found here. We

163

might be arrested for trespassing! Let's slip down cellar and out through the window, and perhaps we can get away without being seen. Never mind the candles! They'll never know who put them there!—Hurry!" She clutched at Cynthia, expecting instant acquiescence. But, to her amazement, Cynthia stood firm, and boldly declared:

"No, Joyce, I'm not going to run away! Even if we got out without being seen, they'd be sure to discover us sooner or later. We've left enough of our things around for that. I'm going to meet whoever it is, and tell them we have n't done any real harm,—and so must you!"

All during this speech they could hear the rattle of some one working at the lock of the main door. And a second after Cynthia finished, it yielded with another loud crack. Next, footsteps were heard in the hall. By this time, Joyce was so paralyzed with fright that she could scarcely move a limb, and speech had entirely deserted her. They were caught as in a trap! There was no escape now. It was a horrible position. Cynthia, however, pulled her to her feet.

"Come!" she ordered. "We'd better meet them and face it out!" Joyce could only marvel at her astonishing coolness, who had always been the most timid and terror-ridden of mortals.

At this instant, the drawing-room door was pushed open!

CHAPTER XIV

THE MEDDLING OF CYNTHIA

TO Joyce, the moment that the drawing-room door was pushed open will always seem, with perhaps one exception, the most intense of all her life. She fully expected to see a man stride in—more likely half a dozen!—and demand the meaning of the unwarrantable intrusion and illumination. Instead of that, the slight figure of a woman dressed all in black, and with a long heavy dark veil over her face, stepped into the room!

For a moment she paused, surprised, uncertain, almost trembling. Then, with a firm movement, she threw back her veil, and, in the soft light of the candles, stood revealed. Joyce gave a tiny gasp. In all her life she had never seen so beautiful an old lady. Masses of soft wavy white hair framed a face of singular charm, despite its age, and the biggest, saddest brown eyes in all the world, looked out inquiringly on the two girls. There was complete silence. The three could hear each other breathe. Then the newcomer spoke:

"Which of you two friends was it, may I ask, who sent me the letter?" Her voice was sweet and low and soft, and as sad as her eyes. Joyce gave a start and opened her lips to speak, but Cynthia was before her.

"*I did!*" she announced calmly. The lady turned to her.

"That was very lovely of you,—and very thoughtful. I began planning to come soon after I received it, and tried to arrive at about the time you mentioned. But I do not quite understand all—all this!" She glanced toward the burning candles. "And I'm afraid I do not understand how you—how you came to be in here!"

"Oh," began Cynthia, stumblingly, "I—I couldn't quite explain it all in a letter—and I didn't even know you'd pay any attention to what I wrote, anyway. But we'll tell you all about it right now, if you care to hear." A light was beginning to dawn on the bewildered Joyce. Suddenly she sprang forward and seized the lady's hand.

"Tell me—oh, please tell me," she cried, *"are* you Mrs. Collingwood?"

"Yes, my dear!" said the lady.

And to the amazement of every one Joyce broke down and began to sob hysterically, exclaiming, "Oh, I'm so glad—so glad!" between every other sob.

"I think I'll sit down," said Mrs. Collingwood, when Joyce had regained control of herself. "I'm very tired—and very, very—bewildered!" She sat down on the sofa, and drew each of the girls down beside her.

"Now tell me," she said to Cynthia. "Explain it all, and then show me what you think will interest me so. You see, I have traveled many weary miles to hear this strange story."

So Cynthia began at the beginning and told how they had first found their way in, and had then become interested in unraveling the mystery of the old house. Mrs. Collingwood listened with deep attention; but when Cynthia reached the tale of the hidden stairway, she started in surprise.

"Why, I never dreamed there was such a thing in the house!" she exclaimed. "The rooms were re-papered once, but I was away when it was done. None of us knew!"

"No, we thought you did n't," continued Cynthia. "And so we went into the locked-up room. And there we found something,—oh!— Mrs. Collingwood! We felt sure you had never seen it, and that you *ought* to! You see, we knew all the rest of the—the story, from Joyce's great-aunt, Lucia Kenway. And we felt you *ought* to see it,—at least *I* felt that way, and so I wrote you the letter. I did n't even tell Joyce I 'd done it, because—because I was afraid she 'd think I was *meddling* in what did n't concern me! But I could n't help it. I could n't sleep nights till I 'd sent that letter, because it all haunted me so! I just sent it to Chesterton, South Carolina, because that was all the address I knew. I did n't even feel sure it would ever reach you.

"And I set a special date for you to get here, on purpose, because—well, because I thought we ought to be here to receive you, and have the place look sort of—homelike. It would be terrible, seems to me, to come back to a dark, deserted house that you'd left so long ago, and nobody here to—to welcome you. Well, that's all, I guess. But Mrs. Collingwood, I'm so afraid we have n't done right,—that we meddled in what was no business of ours, and trespassed in a house we should never have entered! I only hope you can forgive us!" Thus ended Cynthia, brokenly, and Mrs. Collingwood put out her hands to take a hand of each girl in her clasp.

"You dear little meddlers!" she exclaimed. "This is all so astonishing to me; but I feel sure, nevertheless, that you have done nothing but good! And now will you—will you show me what you spoke of?"

Cynthia rose, handed her a lighted candle, and led her to the opening of the little stairway in the library. "It's up these stairs, in the room above—on the desk," she said. "You will find it all lit up there. And I think that—you would rather go—alone!" Mrs. Collingwood took the candle, and Cynthia helped her into the opening at the foot of the stairs. Then she went back to Joyce.

When they were alone, the two girls stood staring at one another and Cynthia's cheeks grew fiery red.

"I don't know what—what you must think of me, Joyce!" she stammered. "I ought never to have done this, I suppose, without telling you."

"Why didn't you tell me?" demanded Joyce.

"Why, I was so afraid you'd think me silly and—and meddling, and you mightn't approve of it. I was unhappy,—I—somehow felt as though I'd committed a crime, and the only way to right it was this!"

"How long ago did you send your letter?" asked Joyce, presently.

Cynthia considered. "I think I posted it a week ago Thursday."

"And you knew all the time, last night, that

this was going to happen to-day?" asked Joyce, incredulously.

"Well, I sort of expected it,—that is, I really did n't know whether she 'd come or not. It made me dreadfully nervous, and that 's the reason I was so cross to you, Joyce, I suppose. Will you forgive me, now that you know?"

"Why, of course!" said Joyce. Then, suddenly, "But, oh!—I *wish* I 'd known this all at the time!"

"What for? What difference would it have made?" demanded Cynthia.

But Joyce only replied: "Hush! Is that Mrs. Collingwood coming down?"

CHAPTER XV

MRS. COLLINGWOOD remained a long time upstairs,—so long, indeed, that the girls began to be rather uneasy, fearing that she had fainted, or perhaps was ill, or overcome—they knew not what.

"Do you think we ought to go up?" asked Cynthia, anxiously. "Perhaps she needs help."

"No, I think she just wants to be by herself. It was fine of you, Cynthia, to send her up alone! I really don't believe I'd have thought of it."

At length they heard her coming slowly down, and presently she reëntered the drawing-room. They could see that she was much moved, and had evidently been crying. She did not speak to them at once, but went and stood by the mantel, looking up long and earnestly at the portrait of the twins.

"My babies!" they heard her murmur unconsciously, aloud. At last, however, she came to them, and sat down once more between them on the sofa. They wondered nervously what she was going to say.

"My little girls—" she began, "forgive me! —you seem little and young to me, though I suppose you consider yourselves almost young ladies; but you see, I am an old woman!—I was going to tell you a little about my life, but I suppose you already know most of the important things, thanks to Great-aunt Lucia!" She patted Joyce's hand.

"There are some things, however, that perhaps you do not know, and, after what you have done for me, you deserve to. I was married when I was a very young girl—only seventeen. I was a Southerner, but my husband came from the North, and brought me up North here to live. I always hated it—this Northern life—and, though I loved my husband dearly, I hated his devotion to it. We

174

never agreed about those questions. When my twin babies were born, I secretly determined that they should be Southerners, in spirit, and *only* Southerners. I planned that when they were both old enough, they should marry in the South and live there—and my husband and I with them.

"But, in this life, things seldom turn out as we plan. My little girl died before she was three; and I had scarcely become reconciled to this grief when my husband was also taken from me. So I centered all my hopes on my son—on Fairfax. As he grew older, however, and as the Civil War came nearer, I noticed that he talked more and more in sympathy with the North, and this distressed me terribly. However, I thought it best not to say much about it to him, for he was a headstrong boy, and had always resented opposition. And I felt sure that he would see things differently when he was older.

"I wished to send him to a Southern college, but he begged me to send him to Harvard. As his heart was so set on it, I could n't deny him,

thinking that even this would make little difference in the end. Then came the crisis in the
country's affairs, and the Confederacy was declared. I had already begun to correspond
with Southern authorities, to arrange about
raising a company for Fairfax. I never
doubted that he would comply with my wishes.
But I little knew him!

"I hardly need to tell you of the awful day
that he came home. You are already acquainted with the history of it. That afternoon, shortly after he arrived, we had our interview. I have always possessed the most
violent temper a mortal had to struggle with.
And in those earlier years, when I got into a
rage, it blinded me to everything else, to every
other earthly consideration. And during that
interview, well,—need I say it?—Fairfax was
simply immovable,—gentle and loving always,
—but I could no more impress him with my
wishes than I could have moved the Rock of
Gibraltar. The galling part to me was—that
he kept insisting he was only doing what was
right! Right?—How *could* he be right when

it was all directly contrary—But never mind that now! I have learned differently, with the passing, sorrowful years.

"But, to go back,—I stood it as long as I could, and then,—I turned from him, disowned him, bade him leave the house at once and never see my face again, and informed him that I myself would abandon the place on the morrow, and return to the South. He left me, without another word, and went to his room. I immediately summoned the servants and dismissed them on the spot, giving them only time to get their things together and go. Then I locked myself in my room till—he was gone. He came several times, knocked at my door, and begged me to see him, but I would not. Heaven forgive me!—I would not! So he must have left me—that note!" She covered her eyes with her hand a moment. Then she went on:

"I never saw or knew of it till this day. If I had—" Just at this point, they were all startled by a loud knock, coming from the direction of the front door. So unexpected was the sound that they could only stare at each other inquiringly without stirring. In a moment it came again,—a thumping of the old knocker on the front inner door.

"I guess I 'd better go," said Joyce. "Some one may have seen the little boarded-up door open—*Did* you leave it open?" she asked, turnto Mrs. Collingwood.

"I think I did. I was too hurried and nervous, when I came in, to think of it."

"That 's it, then. Some one has seen it open, and has stopped to inquire if everything is all right." She hurried away to the front door, and, after an effort, succeeded in pulling it open. A man—a complete stranger to her—stood outside. They regarded each other with mutual surprise.

"Pardon me!" he said. "But perhaps you can inform me—is any one living in this house at present?"

"Why, no!" replied Joyce, rather confusedly. "That is—no, the house is empty, except just—just to-day!"

"Oh! er—I see! The fact is," the stranger

went on, "I was passing here and noticed this outer door open, which seemed a little queer. I used to know the people who lived here—very well indeed—and I have been wondering whether the house was still in their possession. It seemed to be untenanted." At his mention of knowing the family, Joyce looked him over with considerably more interest. He was tall, straight and robust, though rather verging on the elderly. His iron-gray hair was crisply curly, and his dark eyes twinkled out from under bushy gray brows. His smile was captivating. Joyce decided at once that she liked him.

"Oh! did you know the family, the—the—"

"Collingwoods!" he supplemented, with his twinkling smile. "Yes, I knew them—quite intimately. Might I, perhaps, if it would not be intruding, come in just a moment to look once more at the old place? That is," he added hastily, seeing her hesitate, "only if it would be entirely convenient! I do not know, of course, why the house is open. Perhaps people are—are about to purchase it."

Joyce was, for a moment, tongue-tied with perplexity. She hated to refuse the simple wish of this pleasant stranger, yet how was she to comply with it, considering the presence of Mrs. Collingwood, and the almost unexplainable position of herself and Cynthia? What would he think of it all! While she was hesitating, an idea came to her.

"There is one of the family here to-day on—on business," she said, at last. "If you will give me your name, I will ask if—that person would like to see you."

"Oh, that is hardly worth while!" he said, hastily. "My name is Calthorpe,—but I'm sure they would n't remember me after all this time, and I do not wish to trouble them." But Joyce had excused herself and turned away, as soon as she heard the name, leaving him standing there. Mrs. Collingwood, however, shook her head when Joyce announced who was outside.

"I do not remember any one named Calthorpe, and I scarcely feel that I can see a stranger now. But we must not be inhospitable. Miss Cynthia and I will go and sit in the library, and you can bring him into the drawing-room a few moments. There is no other part of the house that can very well be shown." She took Cynthia's arm, walked into the library, and partly closed the door, while Joyce went out to admit the stranger.

"If you care to look around the drawing-room, you will be most welcome," she announced politely. He accepted the invitation gratefully, and entered with her. At the first glance, however, he started back slightly, as with a shock of surprise.

"Why, how strange—how very singular!" he murmured. "These candles—everything— everything just the same as though it were yesterday!"

"Did you often come here?" inquired Joyce. "You must be very well acquainted with the house!"

"Yes. I came often. I was almost like an inmate." He began to wander slowly about the room, examining the pictures. In front of the baby twins he paused a long time.

"Then you must have known young Mr. Fairfax very well," suggested Joyce. "That's he, on the right in the picture." The stranger eyed her curiously.

"Why, yes, I knew him well. But you, little lady, seem quite intimate with the Collingwood family history. Tell me, are you a—a relative?" This confused Joyce anew.

"Oh, no! Just a—just a friend!" she explained. "But I have been told a good deal about them."

"An unhappy family!" was his only comment, and he continued his tour around the room. In front of the old, square, open piano he paused again, and fingered the silk scarf that had, at some long ago date, been thrown carelessly upon it. Then he ran his fingers lightly over the yellow keys. The tones were unbelievably jangling and discordant, yet Joyce thought she caught the notes of a little tune. And in another moment he broke into the air, singing softly the opening line:—

"There never was a sweetheart like this mother fair of mine!—"

THE STRANGER AT THE DOOR

He had sung no more when the face of Mrs. Collingwood appeared in the doorway. Her eyes were wide and staring, her features almost gray in color.

"Who—who *are* you?" she demanded, in a voice scarcely louder than a whisper. The stranger gazed at her with a fixed look.

"Arthur—Arthur Calthorpe!" he faltered.

"No—you are not!"

They drew toward each other unconsciously, as though moving in a dream.

"No one—no one ever knew that song but—" Mrs. Collingwood came closer, and uttered a sudden low cry:

"My son!"

"Mother!"

The two girls, who had been watching this scene with amazement unutterable, saw the strange pair gaze, for one long moment, into each other's eyes. Then, with a beautiful gesture, the man held out his arms. And the woman, with a little gasp of happiness, walked into them!

CHAPTER XVI

JOYCE EXPLAINS

"JOYCE, will you just oblige me by pinching me—real hard! I'm perfectly certain I'm not awake!"

Joyce pinched, obligingly, and with vigor, thereby eliciting from her companion a muffled squeak. The two girls were sitting on the lower step of the staircase in the dark hallway. They had been sitting there for a long, long while.

It was Joyce who had pulled Cynthia away from staring, wide-eyed, at the spectacle of that marvelous reunion. And they had slipped out into the hall unobserved, in order that the two in the drawing-room might have this wonderful moment to themselves. Neither of them had yet sufficiently recovered from her amazement to be quite coherent.

184

"I can't make anything out of it!" began Cynthia, slowly, at last. *"He's dead!"*

"Evidently he is n't," replied Joyce, "or he would n't be here! But oh!—it's true, then! I hardly dared to hope it would be so! I'm *so* glad I did it!" Cynthia turned on her.

"Joyce Kenway! *What* are you talking about? It sounds as though you were going crazy!"

"Oh, of course you don't understand!" retorted Joyce. "And it's your own fault too. I'd have been glad enough to explain, and talk it over with you, only you were so hateful that I just went home instead, and thought it out myself."

"Well, I may be stupid," remarked Cynthia, "but for the life of me I can't make any sense out of what you 're saying!"

"Listen, then," said Joyce, "and I 'll explain it all. You remember last night how I sat reading the newspaper,—first, just to tease you, and afterward I really got interested in it? Well, I happened to be glancing over the news about people who had just landed here

185

from abroad, when a little paragraph caught
my eye. I can't remember the exact words,
but it was something like this,—that among the
passengers just arrived in New York on the
Campania was Mr. *Fairfax Collingwood,* who
was interested in Western and Australian gold
mines. He had not been here in the East for
nearly forty years, and it said how astounded
he was at the remarkable changes that had
taken place during his long absence. Then it
went on to say that he was staying at the Wal-
dorf-Astoria for only a few days, as he was
just here on some important business, and was
then going to cross the continent, on his way
back to Australia.

"Well, you'd better believe that I nearly
jumped out of my skin at the name—Fairfax
Collingwood. It's an unusual one, and it
did n't seem possible that more than one person could have it, though of course it might be
a distant connection of the same family. And
then, too, *our* Fairfax Collingwood was dead.
I did n't know what to think! I tried to get
your attention, but you were still as mad as

you could be, so I made up my mind I'd go home and puzzle over it by myself, and I took the paper with me.

"After I got home, I sat and thought and *thought!* And all of a sudden it occurred to me that perhaps he was n't killed in the war after all,—that there'd been some mistake. I've read that such things did happen; but if it were so, I could n't imagine why he did n't go and make it up with his mother afterward. It seemed very strange. And then this explanation dawned on me,—he had left that note for his mother, and perhaps thought that if she really intended to forgive him, she'd have made some effort to get word to him in the year that elapsed before he was reported killed. Then, as she never did, he may have concluded that it was all useless and hopeless, and he'd better let the report stand, and he disappear and never come back. You see that article said he had n't been East here for forty years.

"And when I'd thought this out, an idea popped into my head. If what I'd imagined was true, it did n't seem *right* to let him go on thinking that, when I knew that his mother never saw that letter, and I decided I 'd let him know it. So I sat right down and wrote a note that went something like this:

"MR. FAIRFAX COLLINGWOOD:

"If you are the same Mr. Fairfax Collingwood who, in 1861, parted from your mother after a disagreement, leaving a note for her which you hoped she would read, I want to tell you that she never saw that note.

"JOYCE KENWAY.

"I signed my name right out, because Father has always said that to write an anonymous letter was the most despicable thing any one could do. And if he ever discovered who I was, I would n't be ashamed to tell him what we had done, anyway. Of course, I ran the chance of his not being the right person, but I thought if that were so, he simply would n't pay any attention to the note, and the whole thing would end there. I addressed the letter to his hotel, and decided that it must be mailed that very night, for he might suddenly leave there and I 'd never know where else to find him. It was then nearly ten o'clock, and I did n't want Father or Mother to know about it, so I teased Anne into running out to the post-office with me. He must have received it this morning."

Cynthia had listened to this long explanation in astonished silence. "Is n't it the most remarkable thing," she exclaimed when Joyce had finished, "that each of us should write, I to the mother and you to the son, and neither of us even guess what the other was doing! And that they should meet here, just this afternoon! But there are a whole lot of things I can't understand at all. Why, for instance, did he give the name of Arthur Calthorpe when he came in, and pretend he was some one else?"

"That's been puzzling me too," replied Joyce, "and I can't think of any reason."

"But the thing that confuses me most of all," added Cynthia, "is this. Why, if you had written that note, and had an idea that he was alive, were *you* so tremendously astonished when he and his mother recognized each other?

189

I should have thought you 'd guess right away, when you saw him at the door, who he was!"

"That's just the queer part of it!" said Joyce. "In the first place, I never expected him to come out here at all,—at least, not right away. I never put the name of this town in the letter, nor mentioned this house. I supposed, of course, that he 'd go piling right down to South Carolina to find his mother, or see whether she was alive. Then, later, when they 'd made it all up (provided she was alive, which even *I* did n't know then), I thought they might come back here and open the house. That was one reason I wanted to have our illumination next week, on the chance of their arriving.

"So you see I was quite unprepared to see him rushing out here at once; and when he gave another name, that completely deceived me. And then, there 's one thing more. Somehow, I had in my mind a picture of Fairfax Collingwood that was as different as could be from— well, from what he is! You see, I 'd always thought of him as the *boy* whom Great-aunt

Lucia described having seen. I pictured him as slim and young looking, smooth-faced, with golden curly hair, and big brown eyes. His eyes are the same but,—well, I somehow never counted on the change that all those forty years would make! You can't think how different my idea of him was, and naturally that helped all the more to throw me off the track."

"But why—" began Cynthia afresh.

"Oh, don't let's try to puzzle over it any more just now!" interrupted Joyce. "My head is simply in a whirl. I can't even *think* straight! I never had so many surprises all at once in my life. I think he will explain everything we don't understand. Let's just wait!"

There were faint sounds from the drawing-room, but they were indistinguishable,—low murmurings and half-hushed sobs. The two reunited ones within were bridging the gulf of forty years. And so the girls continued to wait outside, in the silence and in the dark.

CHAPTER XVII

IN WHICH ALL MYSTERIES ARE SOLVED

AT last the two on the staircase heard footsteps approaching the door, and a pleasant voice called out:

"Where are you both, little ladies? Will you not come and join us? I think we must have some things to be explained!" They came forward, a little timidly, and their latest visitor held out a hand to each.

"You wonderful two!" he exclaimed. "Do you realize that, had it not been for you, this would never have happened? My mother and I owe you a debt of gratitude beyond all expressing! Come and join us now, and we will solve the riddles which I 'm sure are puzzling us all." He led them over to the sofa, and placed them beside his mother.

Never was a change more remarkable than that which had come upon Mrs. Collingwood.

Her face, from being one of the saddest they had ever seen, had grown fairly radiant. She looked younger, too. Ten years seemed suddenly to have dropped from her shoulders. Her brown eyes flashed with something of their former fire, and she smiled down at them as only the Lovely Lady of the portrait had ever smiled. There was no difficulty now in identifying her with that picture.

"Oh, please—" began Joyce, breathlessly, "won't you tell us, Mr. Collingwood, how you come to be—*not dead!*—and why you gave another name at the door—and—and—" He laughed.

"I'll tell you all that," he interrupted, "if you'll tell *me* who 'Joyce Kenway' is!"

"Why, *I* am!" said Joyce in surprise. "Didn't you guess it?"

"How could I?" he answered. "I never supposed it was a *girl* who sent me that note. I did not even feel sure that the name was not assumed to hide an identity. In fact, I did not know what to think. But I'll come to all that in its proper place. I'm sure you are all anxious to hear the strange story I have to tell.

"In the first place, as it's easy to guess, I was n't killed at the battle of Shiloh at all,—but so very seriously wounded—that I came to be so reported. As I lay on the field with scores of others, after the battle, a poor fellow near me, who had been terribly hurt, was moaning and tossing. My own wound did not hamper me so much at the time, so I crawled over to him and tried to make him as comfortable as possible till a surgeon should arrive. Presently he began to shiver so, with some sort of a chill, that I took off my coat and wrapped it round him. The coat had some of my personal papers in it, but I did not think of that at the time.

"When the surgeons did arrive, we were removed to different army hospitals, and I never saw the man again. But he probably died very soon after, and evidently, finding my name on him, in the confusion it was reported that *I* was dead. Well, when I saw the notice of my own death in the paper, my first impulse was to deny it at once. But my second thought was to let it pass, after all. I believed that I had broken forever with my home. In the year that had elapsed, I had never ceased to hope that the note I left would soften my mother's feelings toward me, and that at least she would send me word that I was forgiven. But the word had never come, and hope was now quite dead. Perhaps it would be kinder to her to allow her to think I was no more, having died in the cause I thought right. The more I thought it over, the more I became convinced that this was the wisest course. Therefore I let the report stand. I was quite unknown where I was, and I decided, as soon as I was able, to make my way out West, and live out my life far from the scenes of so much unhappiness. My wound disqualified me from further army service and gave me a great deal of trouble, even after I was dismissed from the hospital.

"Nevertheless, I worked my way to the far West, partly on foot and partly in the slow stage-coaches of that period. Once in California, I became deeply interested in the gold mines, where I was certain, like many another deluded one, that I was shortly going to amass an enormous fortune! But, after several years of fruitless search and fruitless toil, I stood as poor as the day I had first come into the region. In the meantime, the fascination of the life had taken hold of me, and I could relinquish it for no other. I had always, from a small child, been passionately fond of adventure and yearned to see other regions and test my fortune in new and untried ways. I could have done so no more acceptably than in the very course I was now pursuing.

"At the end of those hard but interesting years in California, rumors drifted to me of golden possibilities in upper Canada, and I decided to try my luck in the new field. The region was, at that time, practically a trackless wilderness, and to brave it at all was considered the limit of folly. That, however, far from deterring me, attracted me only the more. I got together an outfit, and bade a`long farewell to even the rough civilization of California.

MYSTERIES ARE SOLVED

"Those were strange years, marvelous years, that I spent in the mountain fastnesses of upper Canada. For month on month I would see no human being save the half-breed Indian guide who accompanied me, and most of the time *he* seemed to me scarcely human. And all the while the search for gold went on, endlessly—endlessly. And the way led me farther and farther from the haunts of men. Then,—one day,—I found it! Found it in a mass, near the surface, and in such quantities that I actually had little else to do but shovel it out, wash it, and lay the precious nuggets aside, till at length the vein was exhausted. On weighing it up, I found such a quantity that there was really no object in pursuing the search any farther. I had enough. I was wealthy and to spare, and the longing came upon me to return to my own kind again. By this time, fifteen years had passed.

"You must not, however, think that in all these years and these absorbing interests, I had forgotten my mother. On the contrary, especially when I was in the wilderness, she was constantly in my thoughts. Before I left California for Canada (the war was then over some four or five years) I had contemplated writing to her, informing her of the mistake about my death, and begging her once more to forgive me. But, for several reasons, I did not do this. In the first place, I had heard of the exceeding bitterness of the South, increased tenfold by the period of reconstruction through which it was then passing. Old grudges, they told me, were cherished more deeply than ever, and members of the same family often regarded each other with hatred. Of what use for me then, I thought, to sue for a reconciliation at such a time.

"Beside that, my very pride was another barrier. I had not been successful. I was, in fact, practically penniless. Would it not appear as though I were anxious for a reconciliation because I did not wish to lose the property which would one day have been mine, had not my mother disinherited me? No, I could never allow even the hint of such a suspicion. I would wait.

MYSTERIES ARE SOLVED

"But, in the Canadian wilderness, I began to see matters in another light. So far from the haunts of humanity and the clash of human interests, one cannot help but look at all things more sanely. It occurred to me that perhaps my mother, far from cherishing any bitter feeling toward me, now that she thought me dead, might be suffering agonies of grief and remorse because we had not been reconciled before the end. If there were even a possibility of this, I must relieve it. So I sat down one day, and wrote her the most loving, penitent letter, begging anew for forgiveness, and giving her the history of my adventures and my whereabouts. This letter I sent off by my guide, to be mailed at the nearest trading-post.

"It took him a month to make the journey there and back. I waited three months more, in great impatience, then sent him back to the same post, to see if there might be a reply. He came back in due time, but bringing nothing for me, and I felt that my appeal had been in vain. Nevertheless, a few months later I wrote again, with no better result. My guide returned empty-handed. And during the last year I was there, I made the third and final trial, and, when again no answer came, I felt that it was beyond all hope to expect forgiveness, since she could ignore three such urgent appeals.

"I have just learned from my mother that these letters were never received by her, which is a great surprise to me, but I think I know the explanation. My guide was not honest,—indeed, few of them are,—but, strangely enough, I never discovered any dishonesty in him, while he was with me. At that time, the postage on letters from that region was very high, sometimes as much as fifty or sixty cents, or even a dollar. This, of course, I always gave to the guide to use in sending the letter when he got to the trading-post. Now, though the sum seems small to us, it was large to him. And though I never suspected it at the time, I have no doubt that he pocketed the money and simply destroyed the letters. So that explains why my mother never received any of them.

MYSTERIES ARE SOLVED

"Well, I returned to California a rich man, able to indulge myself in any form of amusement or adventure that pleased me. I found that I still felt the lure of foreign countries, and the less explored or inhabited, the better. I shipped for a voyage to Japan and China, and spent several more years trying to penetrate the forbidden fastnesses of Tibet. From there, I worked down through India, found my way to the South Sea Islands, and landed at length in Australia with the intention of penetrating farther into that continent than any white man had yet set foot.

"I think by this time, I had pretty well lost all desire ever to return to America, especially to New York. But at intervals I still felt an inexpressible longing to see or hear from my mother. Ten or twelve added years had slipped by, and it did not seem human that she should continue to feel bitterly toward me. I had almost decided to write to her once more, when in Sydney, New South Wales, where I happened to be looking over the files of an old New York paper in the public library, I stumbled on the death-notice of a Mrs. Fairfax Collingwood of Chesterton, South Carolina. The paper was dated seven years before.

"The knowledge was like a knife-wound in my heart. There could be no doubt of the truth. I knew of no other of that name, and the town was the very one in which she lived. My mother now tells me that she knew of this mistake, an error of the New York paper in copying the item from a Southern journal. As a matter of fact, it was a very distant cousin of hers who had died, a Mrs. Fanshawe Collingwood, who also lived in the town. She was my mother's only living relative, and the paper mentioned this circumstance. But when the New York paper copied it, they left out all about the surviving cousin, and merely mentioned the name of the deceased as 'Mrs. Fairfax Collingwood.' My mother had this rectified in a later publication of the paper, but that, of course, I never saw.

"Well, I went into the heart of Australia under the impression that I was now really motherless, and under that impression I have lived ever since. I cannot now detail to you all my wanderings and adventures. I will only say that I became deeply interested in the Australian gold mines, bought up one finally, and have superintended its running ever since. Lately, it became necessary for me to make a business trip to New York in connection with this mine, and I decided to come by way of Europe, since I had never seen that portion of the globe. My business would not keep me in New York more than a week, and I intended to travel at once back to Australia across the continent, in order to see the changes that had taken place since I left.

"I had absolutely no idea of visiting this old home. Why, indeed, should I? My mother, as I supposed, was dead. Nothing else mattered. I had no interest in the property. For aught I knew it might have changed hands twenty times since we lived there. It might not even be in existence.. At any rate, I had no wish to revive the bitterness of that memory. Then came the strange note this morning, which I believe you, Miss Joyce, are responsible for!

"To say that I was completely bewildered by it, would be putting it mildly. It made a statement that was new to me, indeed, and might account for many things. But what was I to do about it? Which way should I turn? No use to hurry down to South Carolina,—my mother being dead. Of whom should I make inquiries? The firm of New York lawyers that I remembered her as formerly retaining, I dreaded to consult, lest they think I had come to make a claim on the property. There seemed to be absolutely no clue.

"And then I happened to look at the envelope and saw that it was postmarked 'Rockridge,' a region which I speedily ascertained was right in the vicinity of my old home. That decided me to come out here at once, this afternoon, hunt up the spot, and try to discover in this way whether there was any use of pursuing investigations further in this direction.

"As I have said, I naturally supposed that the property had changed hands many times before this; and that all its old belongings had long since been sent to my mother or sold by her orders.

"When I arrived in this street and saw the old house still standing, forlorn, unkempt, apparently deserted, and quite unchanged since I knew it, I was still more astonished. But when I noticed the little door in the boarding standing open, I resolved to begin my investigations right there, and I boldly went up and knocked. Then Miss Joyce came out and announced that a member of the Collingwood family was here on business. That, too, seemed incredible, as I remembered no surviving member of the family. Discretion, however, seemed to me the better part of valor, and I decided to give the name that I had borne during my first years in California, till I could ascertain more definitely just what the situation was.

"So I came in—as Mr. Arthur Calthorpe—and the mystery deepened tenfold when I saw this old room all lit up precisely as I had remembered it so many years ago. It so carried me back into my youth that, for a few moments, I quite lost track of the present. And when I came to the old piano, the impulse seized me to play a few bars and hum the lines of a little song I had once composed for my mother. I had at that time rather a gift for music, and this song was a sort of secret of ours—I never sang or played it for any one else. And she remembered it!

"Well, you know the rest!—" And he stopped abruptly. They all drew long breaths of relaxed tension.

"There 's something that has puzzled me all along," began Joyce, at last. "I wonder if Mrs. Collingwood would object to my asking about it?"

"No, indeed, dear child," replied that lady. "Have no hesitation in asking what you wish."

"It 's this, then. I have often and often wondered why you never came back to this beautiful old home, or at least sent for the books and pictures and lovely things that were going to ruin here. Did you never think of it?"

"I do not wonder that you ask," answered Mrs. Collingwood, "for it must have seemed very strange to an outsider. Of course, for the first few years, my anger had been so great, and my grief was still so terrible, that I felt I could never, never look upon the place or anything in it again. Then, as you have heard, I willed the house itself and the land to the Southern Society, as I had no one to whom I wished to leave it, and my means were sufficient, so that I did not need to sell it. As the years passed on, however, and my feelings altered, I did begin to think it a pity that the place should run to neglect and ruin.

"So strong did this conviction become, that I decided to come North myself, and personally superintend putting the house in order. I could not bear to leave this task to outsiders. I even thought that, if I found I could endure the memories, I would live in it a while, for the sake of the old happy years with my little boy. I even had my trunks packed and my ticket bought, when suddenly I came down with typhoid fever, so severe an attack that it was thought I could not live. That ended all thoughts of my coming North for a long while, as I was miserably weak and helpless for months after, and in fact, have never quite recovered my strength. The years drifted on and with them came old age, and the reluctance to make the long journey and endure the strain of it all. Had it not been for Miss Cynthia's letter, I should never have come.

"But, to change the subject a trifle, my son is very anxious to know how you two young things have come to be concerned in all this, and I have not yet had time to tell him—fully. Will you not give him an account of it now? It is very wonderful."

And so they began, first Joyce and then Cynthia,—interrupting and supplementing each other. They were still rather anxious on the subject of meddling and trespassing, but they did not try to excuse themselves, recounting the adventures simply and hiding nothing. The older people listened intently, sometimes amused, sometimes touched, often more deeply moved than they cared to show.

MYSTERIES ARE SOLVED

"We began it at first just for fun,—we pretended to be detectives. But as it went on, we got more and more deeply interested, till at last this—this all seemed more important than our own lives," ended Joyce. "Only, I know we did wrong in the beginning ever to come in here at all. We are trespassers and meddlers, and I hope you can forgive us!"

"The dearest little meddlers in the world!" cried Mrs. Collingwood. "Can any forgiveness be necessary?" And she cuddled them both in her arms.

"There's just one thing *I'd* like to ask, if you don't mind," said Cynthia, coming suddenly out of a brown study. "It's the one thing we never could account for. Why was that room upstairs locked, and what has become of the key?" Mrs. Collingwood flushed.

"I locked the door and threw the key down the well—that night!" she answered slowly. "I don't suppose you can quite understand, if you are not afflicted with a passionate temper, as I was. When my son—when Fairfax here —had gone, and I was shutting up the house

and came to his room,—I wanted to go in,—
oh, you cannot know how I wanted to go in!
But I knew that if I once entered and stood
among his dear belongings, I should relent—
I should rush away to find him and beg him
to come back to me. And I—I did not *want*
to relent! I stood there five minutes debating
it. Then I suddenly locked the door on the
outside, and before giving myself time for a
second thought, I rushed downstairs, out of
doors, and threw the key into the old well,—
where I could never get it again!

"Children, I am an old woman. I shall be
seventy-five next birthday. Will you heed a
lesson I have learned and paid for with the
bitterest years of my life? If you are blessed
with a calm, even, forgiving nature, thank God
for it always. But if you are as I was, pray
daily for help to curb that nature, before you
have allowed it to work some desperate evil!"
She hid her face in her hands.

"There, there, little Mother of mine!" murmured her son. "Let us forget all that now!
What does anything matter so long as we are

together again—for always?" He leaned over, pulled her hands from her face, and kissed her tenderly. The moment was an awkward one, and Cynthia wished madly that she had not been prompted to ask that unfortunate question. Suddenly, however, the tension was broken by Mrs. Collingwood exclaiming:

"Mercy me! See that enormous *cat* walking in! Wherever did it come from?" They all turned toward the door.

"Oh, that's Goliath!" said Joyce, calmly. "He feels very much at home here, for he has come in with us often. He led the way that first day, if you remember. And he's been *such* a help!— He's a better detective than any of us!"

"Blessings on Goliath then, say I!" laughed Mr. Fairfax Collingwood, and, approaching the huge feline with coaxing words, he gathered its unresisting form in his arms and deposited the warm, furry purring beast in his mother's lap.

And while they were all laughing over and petting Goliath, a queer thing happened. The candles, which had been burning now for several hours, had, unnoticed by all, been gradually guttering and spluttering out. At length only four or five flames remained, feebly wavering in their pools of melted wax. The occupants of the room had been too absorbed with their own affairs to notice the gradual dimming of the illumination. But now Joyce suddenly looked up and perceived what had happened.

"Why, look at the candles!" she cried. "There are only about three left, and they won't last more than a minute or two!" Even as she spoke, two of them flickered out. The remaining one struggled for another half-minute, and flared up in one last, desperate effort. The next instant, the room was in total darkness. So unexpected was the change, that they all sat very still. The sudden pall of darkness in this strange house of mystery was just a tiny bit awesome.

"Well! This *is* a predicament!" exclaimed Fairfax Collingwood who was first to recover from the surprise. "Fortunately I have a box of matches!"

Then, with one accord they began to steer their **way**
around the furniture

"Oh, don't worry!" added the practical Cynthia. "There's an extra candle that I left on the mantel. It will do nicely to light us out." Groping to the chimney-place with the aid of his matches, Mr. Collingwood found the candle and lit it. Then, with one accord, they all rose and began to steer their way around the furniture toward the hall, Goliath following. In the hall, Mr. Collingwood looked at his watch, exclaiming:

"It is six-thirty! Who would believe it!" The two girls gave a simultaneous gasp of dismay.

"Dinner!—It was ready half an hour ago! What *will* they think?" cried Joyce.

"Never mind *what* they think, just for to-night!" responded Mrs. Collingwood, gaily. "You can tell them when you're explaining all this, that what you've done for us two people is beyond the power of words to express. They'll forgive you!" She bent down and kissed them both with a caress that thrilled them to their finger-tips. Then they all passed out through the great front door to the wide old veranda. Mr. Collingwood, taking the key from his mother, locked the little door in the boarding, after them. And in the warm, waning May afternoon, they filed down the steps. At the gate, Mr. Collingwood turned to the girls:

"I am taking my mother back to New York for a few days. She must rest, and we have much to talk over. I scarcely need tell you that I am *not* returning to Australia!—We shall come back here very soon, open up this old home, put it in order, and probably spend the rest of our lives between here and the South.

"Dear girls, I hardly need say to you that in all the world we shall consider that we have no closer or more devoted friends than yourselves! This house will always be open to you. You must look upon it as a second home. You have given back to us the most priceless blessing,—the one thing we neither hoped nor expected to enjoy again in this world,—*each other!*" He could not go on. He was very much moved. And as for the two girls, they were utterly speechless under the pressure of feeling.

They remained standing at the gate, watching the two go down the street in the sunset, and waved to them wildly as they turned to look back, just before rounding the corner. And at last the intervening trees shut them from sight.

When they were gone, Cynthia and Joyce turned and looked long and incredulously into each other's eyes. They *might* have made, on this occasion, a number of high-flown and appropriate remarks, the tenor of which would be easy to imagine. Certainly the time for it was ripe, and beyond a doubt they *felt* them! But, as a matter of fact, they indulged in nothing of the sort. Instead, Joyce suddenly broke into a laugh.

"We 'll never have to go in there by the cellar window again!" she remarked.

"Sure enough!" agreed Cynthia. "What a relief that 'll be!"

And so ended the adventure of the Boarded-up House!